Rite of Passage

New Earth Series Volume I

T.K. TENIEL

Rite of Passage / New Earth Series Volume I / 2

To my love…..Thank you for pushing me to be the best person I can be. And for showing me that it's okay to share that person with the world.

Chapter 1

Leaves rustle under my feet as I sprint through the forest. My heart beating rhythmically with every stride. I jump over a fallen tree in front of me with the ferocity of a panther; never once taking my eyes off my prey. I slow my pace to a long stride and creep closer to my opponent. Slowly and carefully, placing one foot in front of the other, as not to disturb the earth below me, I kneel next to a large moss covered stone.

Removing the bow from my back, fashioned from the spine of a bear that my father made for me on my 17th year, I quietly placed the arrow on the rest. Taking a deep breath I aim, studying the jaguar as she eats her rabbit.

The rabbit I'd planted and had been tracking for two days in hopes that it would lure that tricky jaguar back to me. I was impatient and too quick to pounce last time. But I know better now and this time she will be mine.

Exhaling, I let go of the string. The arrow slices thru the crisp air hitting the jaguar directly in the heart.

Zeke would be proud. He taught me everything I know about the hunt. I caught on quickly too! He called me a natural. After he went missing two years ago, I was nominated by my tribe to step up and become the new hunter. My father isn't quite as young as he used to be, and it is our tribes' responsibility to provide for our caste. It was my 16th year when I accepted the honor, and let me tell you, it hasn't been an easy job to uphold. This is the first big piece of meat I've been able to bring home in months. Our meals have consisted of fish, fruits, vegetables and small animals like rabbits and lizards; with the occasional piece of bread. And though I'm grateful for what I've been able to bring home, I'm elated at the thought of having a real meal tonight. The victory of every kill brings me a little comfort knowing my brother still lives on through me.

Zeke's disappearance devastated our village and forced my mother into a deep depression. We scoured the woods for weeks, looking for any trace of him when he didn't come home after hunting that day. After a month, the council concluded that my brother must have been hunted and killed by some members of the Silliloqui tribe and had a funeral to put him to rest. I was unconvinced. Even with the confirmation of the Janti tribe leader Chenoa, I'd much rather believe that he fell in love and ran away one day. Choosing to be free beyond these villages that we've created.

That's what allows me to sleep at night.

I place one hand over the jaguar's eyes and the second on the arrow. "Amoke Len greth, suni lemye (from your death, comes life)", and removed the arrow. Hoisting the jaguar onto my shoulders I began the hike home.

Although I was lean and feminine like my mother, I possessed the power and strength of my father. Easily beating the boys of my village in everything from hunting to academics. My father wouldn't accept anything less. "*A lazy body is a dead body.*" He used to say when I complained about waking up so early for lessons.

My brother on the other hand was always concerned that my competitive nature would make it impossible for me to marry one day. *'Never be too proud to loose, no man wants a wife that is too strong. It's intimidating.'* In which I would respond *'Who needs a man? I can do everything a man can do, and better!'* At that, he would just shake his head and say *'You'll see one day, no matter how strong you are, you will always need a balance. Masculine and feminine energy is what makes this world what it is, and one cannot exist without the other.'* I'm still trying to understand what he meant by that, but out of respect for his wisdom, I do try a lot harder to stay humble.

I do enjoy my solitude though so it'll probably be a while before I settle down and become someone's wife. I can't imagine sharing my peaceful hunting trips with anyone other than my brother. The smells and sounds of the wildlife are a constant reminder of Mother Earth's everlasting beauty. Always changing, growing, moving, and sometimes dying life followed me with every step. Tonight seemed especially peculiar because the fireflies lit the path home.

Stepping on the rocks in the shifting stream I could see the smoke rising from the freshly started fires in my village ahead.

The children are immersed in a game of freeze tag, completely ignoring the scolds of the elders. My mother's gazing at my father as he sits next to her telling tales of his youth to the other tribe members. No matter how many times he tells those stories, my mother always listens earnestly like it is her first time hearing them. And I wonder if I will ever look at someone the way she looks at him.

The children see me coming up the path and run to meet me. Smiling and wide eyed at the sight of the jaguar I balance on my shoulders.

"Zee das fane! Zee das fane! (Put it down)" they chant, laughing loudly.

I place our feast on the pile of leaves next to the one of the fire pits and the children skip around and sing praises to The Mother for our nourishment.

My mother, Aquene, turns her attention at sound of the chants and walks over to greet me. Smiling, she grabs my face with both hands and kisses my forehead.

"Greetings my love. I see the Gods have blessed us with a feast before your big day tomorrow."

"Greetings Mother" I say smiling back at her. "Thank you for your kind words. How have you been today?"

"I've been blessed my child. My…" she pauses, searching for the right word, "health…. matters not to me." she says finally "I ask only for blessings for you on your journey tomorrow."

She still struggles with the language of the old world. Being raised during the war, she was taught Phipsi, the language of our surviving caste. A language that was created to align the people who had the same belief system about Mother Earth; That it's to be protected and cared for, not taken advantage of.

"Thank you mother." I say and kiss her hands with gratitude. A village elder calls her over to help prepare dinner and she pats my hand and makes her way over to the serving table.

My father still sits by the fire telling his story, but looks over at me and smiles, acknowledging my return. His voice was prominent and seemed to vibrate through the village. I walk over and wait patiently for him to finish. He laughs heartily at his own jokes and talks for at least 5 more minutes before finishing his story and redirecting his attention to me.

His tall stature towers over my frame as he stands to kiss my forehead. "Many blessings to you child." he says and sits back on the log to rest. "The gods must look down on you with favor this evening!" his warm baritone voice filling me like a hot cup of tea.

"I pray that it keeps us healthy!" I say, dutifully.

"Come my child, you have been gone all day. Sit and tell me of your adventures!" he says, beaming with pride.

"Well father, there isn't much to tell." I sit next to him on the log. "I spent the day in the forest, eating berries, hunting, talking to the butterflies, you know, the usual."

He laughs "Talking to butterflies you say, and what do they have to say?" his eyes wide and eager like that of a young child.

I bite my lip fearing I've said too much. But he is in a good mood today, maybe this time it will be different.

"Well, not much, they're usually shy creatures, but one told me how her daughter just came out of her cocoon this morning! All of the butterflies rejoiced because they thought she wouldn't make it because she was sick. I had no doubts though. She's a fighter! And sure enough, she spread her beautiful orange and black wings today. It was quite the sight." I say, excited to share the good news.

His eyes glaze over and he stares at me with that look I dread. My blood runs cold and I immediately regret telling him about my experience. Stupid Zaphora and your eternal optimism. Why would today be any different? He'll always look at you this way, ashamed of the daughter that can hear the animals.

"You my dear have quite the imagination." he says, wiping a tear that has fallen. "Wash up now and get ready for dinner."

He stables himself on his wooden cane and limps over to our hut, closing the door behind him.

Frustration overcomes me and I try my best to suppress it. These are the times I really miss Zeke. I would tell him of my adventures and he never used to make me feel this way. But every time I've tried to bring it up to my father, he always looks at me with disappointment in his eyes. The first time I told him he shook the table we were sitting at with fury and yelled for me to never say such things to anyone else. He doesn't want to be known as the chief with the crazy daughter who thinks she can talk to animals. But I know what I feel. What I hear. I'm not crazy….am I?

Later that night I lie awake staring at the mosquito flying around the net covering my cot. My black and russet colored locks lay wildly on the pillow away from my face, giving me a false illusion of coolness on this humid night. My 18th year is tomorrow and it'll be my turn to embark on my Spirit Journey.

A tradition that was implemented in our New Earth after the Great War of Venus in the year 2020. A war that lasted 100 years and destroyed most of our natural resources.

There is some talk about how there might be another reason why the Spirit journey was created. There are stories of another tribe known as the Silliloquii tribe that was banished many years ago because they resorted to cannibalism when they felt as if they weren't eating enough. It is said that the elders feared that if not given the proper guidance, we too might fall victim to the same fate. Thus the Spirit Journey was born. A voyage to insure the survival of our tribes by making sure that we stay connected to the Mother and our essence.

Whatever the reason for its creation the one thing that is definite is that everyone's journey is different and can last anywhere from 10 days to 20 years, depending on how quickly you learn the lessons that your Spirit Journey provides.

My anticipation rises and falls with each breath I take. It worries me that it will take longer than expected to complete this journey, and with my father's failing health, I want to make sure that I'm here if anything happens to him. My mother can't take another heartbreak. She wouldn't survive it.

After tossing and turning for another hour in the humidity, I decide to start my day early and take a run to warm up my muscles. My mother is easily awoken so I had to learn at an early age how to be like a shadow when moving through the house after certain hours. Her insomnia didn't begin until after my brother disappeared and I'll have to suffer the wrath of my father if I wake her.

I turn the knob on the wooden door and crack it open just enough so I'm able to slide out. Mastery.

The moon gives way to the coming sun as I take off into the forest. This hour is the most peaceful for me. While all the world is asleep and I can take in the beauty of nature undisturbed.

I arrive back to the village as the sun is beginning to rise. The kids were already up and running around and the villagers from the Janti and Xouxi tribes are already arriving. The smell of the ceremonious pig is being roasted over the fire makes my stomach growl with delight. I guess I wasn't the only one anticipating my journey today.

Chapter 2

"Zaphora, my dear. Come and eat. Zwa shai stee vlag rogjay. (You only have a short while to get ready.)" My mother says, placing pieces of ham in bowls at the beginning of the line.

"Thank you mother. I will" I kiss her on the cheek and follow the bowl down the line until I reach my aunt Jaylene, who puts some chopped up pears in the bowl and hands it to me. I find a seat near my uncle Ashanti, who is going on about his own spirit journey, when I realize that I forgot to pack and make my way to my room instead.

Stuffing a piece of ham in my mouth, I look up to see my mother shaking her head from afar in disapproval. *'Eat like a lady Zaphora, I didn't raise you to be anything less than.'* I can hear her say. I swallow the ham and decide to wait until I get to my room to eat in order to avoid any more unwanted glares.

I decide to take my favorite bag made of wolf hide, one of the few items I still have of my brothers, and pack my throwing knives, snake skin jacket, some underwear, bandages, and a couple of rose water vials (to help fight infection should anything happen).

I consume the eggs, toast, pears and rest of the ham in my bowl with ease. Tossing the bowl into the sink. An unpleasant fragrance of must and woods fills my nostrils with each movement, so I decide to wash up before heading back out to the ceremony. I open the bathroom door to see a bath already made for me in our makeshift wooden tub. A smile spreads across my face as I think about how thoughtful and intuitive my mother is. I take my time bathing and washing my locks. Not knowing when the next bath will find me. When I finally pry myself out of the now cool water, I decide to wear a dark green tank and cargo pants for my trip today. A look I've been planning since my 15th year. It reminds me of the pictures I used to study of the solders of the old world. One of my reminders to keep myself focused on the task at hand.

I place my backpack and arrows over my shoulder; grabbing my bow on the way out the door.

"Lowhi Zaphora! Today's the big day! You nervous? You think you gonna take 20 years to find your destiny? Huh? Huh?" Sasha says running at my side. I'm starting to regret teaching her the language of the old world. I love her but her eagerness and 50 questions are not what I need as I prepare for this journey.

"Sasha sweetie, I am in need of time for self-reflection, would you do me the honor of granting that time please?" I say as politely as a can through clenched teeth.

"Sure big cousin! I mean, of course I will grant you the time you need, it would be my honor." She hugs my waist and runs quickly to play with the other children. Her sandy brown braids bouncing with glee.

I look toward the center of the village and see the men are taking turns throwing logs and brush into a pit, setting up the big fire for the ceremony.

I'm filled with a nervous energy as I make my way towards a group of my friends hanging out by the well. My eyes roam and lock on a tall man standing near Asta, the leader of the Xouxi tribe. His hair is long and locked, tied securely behind his head. His eyes are pools of almond dreams sitting perfectly on chocolate skin. He towers over Asta at least 2 feet but they share the same broad nose and confident, regal posture. He looks like, but it can't be………..Makiya?

He smiles and starts walking towards me, the tribal tattoo of a hawk on his right arm catching my eye for a quick moment. I'm so enamored with him that I have stopped in my tracks. I quickly blink away my trance and continue towards the well.

"Lowhi, mi swasta shen Makiya (Hi, my name is Makiya)." He says, extending his hand toward mines.

"Makiya? It's me Zaphora! I'm sorry, I mean Makiya shaul mi swasta shen Zaphora." I say, trying to hide my uneasiness in his presence.

"Zaphora? Wow. It's been a long time!" he says, embracing me in his huge arms, lingering a bit before letting me go.

"I should have known it was you with those beautiful gray eyes. So are you still kicking butt and taking names?"

"Well, I do what I can." I say shyly. Reminiscing on the classes we use to have together.

That was before our leaders decided that they could build stronger members of the community by teaching their children what was important to their own tribe as soon as possible; which left behind most of the academic learning and focused more on each tribes Nature Given abilities. Since I was 10 years old when this change occurred I was able to experience the effects of both methods. And between me and you, I think we made stronger members of the community when we were together, and learning about the past instead of just the present and future. You can't know where you've going until you know where you've been.

I look towards the fire and he follows my gaze.

"So you're what all the commotion is about. Are you excited about you're spirit journey?"

"Yes. But I'm not sure how prepared I am. Especially since I don't know what to expect." I don't know why I said that. I have been keeping my feelings to myself about this journey, so what made me want to tell him?

"Well, there is nothing for you to be intimidated about. You seem like the type of woman that is in tune with her soul, and that's all the preparation you need. Just listen, and you will be guided where you need to go." He says with a smile, engulfing me in his gaze again.

 A woman. No one has ever called me a woman before. I guess today is the beginning of my womanhood. I spent so much time trying to be the boy my father lost that I hadn't recognized that I've indeed become a woman. His words gave me a confidence I didn't have when I awoke this morning and I wish that I could talk to him more.

Asta looks over at us and Makiya brakes his gaze to look back at him. "Umm, I've got to get back. But good luck to you Zaphora, not like you'll need it or anything. I'm sure you'll put us all to shame, like you usually do." he says with a smirk before jogging back over to Asta.

Butterflies have a party in my stomach as I continue walking to the water well. I don't remember feeling this way about Makiya the last time I saw him. He has always been like a second brother to me. But this time it's different. His touch makes my skin feel hot and tingly. What is happening to me?

"Gather around brothers and sisters. Thank you all for coming out to yet another Spirit Journey." Lemak says over the many small conversations. Deciding to speak in the language of the old world based on the demographic of the crowd.

Everyone quickly moves into silence at the sound of his voice before he continues. "Today is a very special day to me because this Spirit Journey will be taken by my beautiful, brave, highly imaginative daughter Zaphora."

The crowd bursts into laughter, and I suddenly feel a little ashamed for sharing so many of my adventures in the forest with my family and friends. I look down and laugh a little, hoping he will get on with his speech already.

"As you all know, our history as a people has been somewhat of a dark one. War and famine ravaged our lands over 100 years ago turning brother against brother, sister against sister, until our Mother cried unto her Earth with a great storm cleansing us from the destruction we'd created and giving us a chance to start anew. But these were trying times, leaders were needed to guide our people in the right direction, and one by one our Mother showed us who those leaders should be. Asta and our deceased sister Chimala, leaders of the Xouxi tribe. Experts of governing our Mother's resources. Ensuring that we shall never take more than what we need or give less than we can offer. Chenoa and Hosa, leaders of he Janti tribe. Our conduits to our deceased brothers and sisters and the healers of our people. Finally there is myself and Aquene of the Seraphine tribe, who, with the help of our fellow tribe members, provides food for our people through our extensive knowledge of hunting and farming. Ensuring that we will never face another famine again.

And through that storm, we rose. A stronger, more grounded people. Humbled by the experience we were fortunate enough to live through, we vowed to give the rest of our lives to the service and preservation of our Mother."

"To only Mother we serve." We all say in unison.

"Zaphora, come to me my dear." He reaches for me and I walk over and put my hand in his. I'll miss his bear like callused hands when I'm away. They feel safe. They feel like home.

"My darling Zaphora, you have grown into a wonderful woman, with the spirit of a warrior, and the strength of a lion." My tribe explodes into chants and screams "Seraphine Sheeth! Seraphine Sheeth! (Seraphine Strong)" My father smiles a broad smile then clears his throat, calming the crown before he continues.

"I have no doubt that this journey will not only bring you closer to your calling, but will also bring pride to our tribe." He lets go of my hands and picks up the metal rod that was sticking out of the fire. Putting the rod in a bowl of tusk nectar, a liquid, sappy substance discovered by the Janti tribe, known to expedite the healing process.

"This symbol marks your allegiance to our tribe, Seraphine. By branding this symbol into your skin, you vow to uphold the laws of the land. Pledging yourself to the development and continuous growth of yourself, the brothers and sisters of our caste, and the one and only Mother Earth; who has spared our lives and allowed us to begin again. Remembering always where we have come from, and advancing our race to a new level of understanding through truth and love. Will you accept this oath?"

Rite of Passage / New Earth Series Volume I / 17

"Yes, I will accept this oath." I say, looking into my father's eyes with both fear and excitement. He smiles back at me, his eyes warm with delight.

He then lifts the metal rod out of the tusk nectar and I see what's on the other end, it's a tribal image of a lion, our tribes' symbol. He pulls my locks back behind my right shoulder and gently places the symbol on my right arm.

The scorching is instant. Hot flesh melts under the rod and I feel as if it will eat away to the bone. Smoke fills my nose and I feel bile creeping its way up my throat. I turn my head and try to focus on my breathing, focus on the sounds of the birds flying above me, on the crackling of the fire, anything but the skin falling off my arm. I look up, trying to blink tears out of my eyes and catch Makiya's gaze. His warm smile swallows me whole for a few seconds and it's over.

Everyone erupts in praise and cheer. My father dips a bandage in rose water, and places it over the brand to seal the burn. I smile and hug my father and mother. My burn stinging under the bandage.

An elder in the crowd starts to sing the Caste song, and everyone joins along joyfully.

"Sha-La ti raq ti, Sha-flowi resi fliq ti, Ja les lowee shi, Ja les lowee liv." (The world couldn't break us, the Mother has awakened us. We serve only her. We serve only love.)..........

Through the melody my mother leans into my ear and whispers "Jaiy singe swan zi phoh mi chi. Twu zhi la vivi suzi. Jian la-kee nwa shosi lami, nawa less zi, nawa less naima." (I'm so proud of you my child. You have become such a beautiful soul.

Remember wherever this journey takes you, never lose that. Never lose your essence.)

She pulls back and kisses me on the cheek. She then hands me a sack made of dear leather and makes room for my father.

"Thank you mother, I appreciate your wisdom." I say smiling; feeling the warmth of her words and embrace.

My father puts his arms around me carefully, as to not touch the tattoo he just branded on my arm.

"I have something that I believe will help you in your journey my daughter." He reaches into his back pocket and takes out a small bag made of bear hide and hands it to me. "Open it."

I unfold it to reveal a collection of handcrafted pocket knives with a Z imprinted in the handle of each.

"As you know, my hands haven't been as steady as they use to be, so I had Asta craft these knives for you to take on your trip." Asta looks over and nods respectively to me, his beady eyes looking like portals to another world. I almost shudder. I nod back and quickly put my focus back on my father.

"Thank you father, they are perfect." I say, taking the knives from him and placing them and my wolf sack into the bag that my mother just gave me.

My fellow tribe members chant and sing as I make my way towards the main road. A chill goes down my spine when I notice Soriya glaring at me through the crowd. Her haunting green eyes watching every step I take. She raises one thinly arched eyebrow when she notices me looking in her direction.

I quickly avert my gaze. The last thing I need before this trip is her altering my aura.

Makiya notices her glare and gives her a light punch in the arm to brake her trance. Maneuvering through a few women and children, he makes his way over to me.

"Don't let her vibe shake you" he says "She just wishes she could have received the same kind of sendoff, you know?"

I did know. The Xouxi tribe sends its members to start their spirit journey in a very different fashion. They are awoken on their 18th year before the sun rises, and sent on their journey with only the clothes on their backs and one weapon. They're not considered official members of their tribe until they make it back from their journey and are branded with their tribes' symbol, a hawk. Their leader, her father, Asta, believes that it allows the traveler to become one with the earth without any distractions. Thus increasing their ability to read auras and allowing them to more accurately identifying their destiny.

"Yes, but that doesn't give her the right to make me feel bad because my tribe chooses to do things differently. I know she's your sister, but sometimes I wonder where all her bad energy comes from." As soon as I say this I stumble on a rock and he helps me regain my balance. I blush looking around to make sure no one saw and catch Soriya glaring at me with a smirk on her face.

"Zaphora" Makiya says braking my gaze "I wanted to tell you….umm, I don't know how to explain it. It's just..." his eyebrows furrow like he's searching for the right words. "Just be careful okay?"

"I always am." I say a matter-of-factly.

"No, I'm serious Zaphora. I don't know what it is. Your aura is not as bright as it usually is, like something's blocking it. Just be careful out there okay?" He says, concern encompassing his tone.

"I will. Thank you for the heads up Makiya. I'll see you in a month, tops!"

"I'm sure you'll do great. Good luck!"

I smile and turn from him, picking up my pace towards the road ahead. Not knowing where this journey will take me, but anticipating it will lead to greatness.

 My greatness.

Chapter 3

It's been hours since I heard the voices of the tribes cheer me into the unknown. The sun is starting to set now and I think I should look for a place to camp for the night.

The musty air sticks to my skin like a wet sweater. The thought of it makes me wish I was at home so I could go to the waterhole and cool off with my friends.

The trees are thick and high, with thin branches, making it impossible to climb and see what's ahead.

Is that a cave? I squint to get a better look in the darkening woods and hear rustling behind me.

Slowly turning my head, I hope whatever is moving behind me will not pounce before I'm able to flee. A cloud of smoke moves through the trees, covering the ground like a wave on the beach. A tall dark figure stands in the smoke for a moment, darts to the right and is gone. Soon after the smoke starts to decapitate as well. I blink my eyes quickly trying to understand what I just saw. I must be getting tired.

With long strides, I make my way toward what I think is a cave in the distance. As I move closer I see vines hanging in front of the cave entrance, with a large rock about 3 feet from the door.

It's not the best accommodations, but its home for the night. And I can definitely use that rock as a chair while I roast one of the rabbits my mother packed in the bag for me.

Reaching the front of the cave I drop my bag next to the rock and reach in to pull out a piece of cloth and a jar of lavender oil.

I squat to get a closer look at the ground beneath me, picking up the greenest, thickest branch that I could find. Securing the cloth around the branch, I carefully open up the jar of lavender oil and dip the cloth side into the jar, making sure that the cloth is completely soaked in oil. I then take out my pocket knife and an old piece of steel and strike the knife against the steel until the spark from the two creates a fire on my makeshift torch. I pick up the branch immediately, not wanting to cause a forest fire and head towards the entrance of the cave.

Pulling back the vines carefully, I wave the torch in first and stand on the outside. Sort of a warning to the current occupants that they have company. A couple of bats fly past my head, and after a couple of seconds I enter the cave. Surprisingly, aside from being small and dusty, it wasn't that bad. No unwanted creatures, besides the usual crawling kind, inhabit the grounds.

I make my way back outside to gather some leaves for my bedding and sticks for the fire I'm about to start. Moving quickly through the woods, I was able to make my pallet and get started on the fire before the sun set. After ensuring that the torch was completely extinguished, I placed it in the bag with my other belongings to be used at a later time.

Relaxing next to the fire after my meal, I try to get lost in the sounds around me. Wolves howl, wood crackles, and crickets chirp. Usually these sounds are soothing and remind me of the camping trips my father used to take me and Zeke on when we were younger. But tonight is different. I can't get what Makiya out of my mind.

'Be careful Zaphora, I'm serious!' Those words play an unsettling song in my head.

Rite of Passage / New Earth Series Volume I / 23

And that figure in the smoke in the woods a couple of hours ago. What was that? Could that have something to do with what he was talking about? Am I being hunted? Or watched? Am I being watched right now? The very thought sends a shiver down my spine and I decide to turn in for the night before my mind gets too carried away.

Lying awake on my makeshift bed I close my eyes and try to get some sleep.

You have a long day ahead of you tomorrow Zaphora.

Focus on your breathing Zaphora. Inhale. Exhale. Nothing else.

Smoke and a dark figure in front of me.

Walking closer. Closer towards me.

It extends what looks like an arm out to me but resembles a tree branch dripping with black tar. The end of the branch touches my cheek and the black liquid spreads over my face. Sealing my mouth. I try to move and feel stiff. I stare at the figure in front of me and it looks almost sympathetic, tilting its head to the side right before the liquid makes its way into my eyes.

Darkness.

I jerk awake and grab at the dirt at my side. Sweat rolling down my face, soaking my back and causing leaves to stick to my shoulders. A bright light shines through the cave entrance, blinding me.

That dream. What the heck was that about?

But I have no time to ponder it now. I have to figure out where that beaming light is coming from if I plan on getting any more rest tonight.

I stand and brush off the leaves that stick to my soaked body. I look around in my bag. Got it. I pull out 2 knives, stick one in my belt and put the other in my left hand.

Putting my other hand up over my face in an attempt to shield my eyes, I walk slowly to the cave opening, trying to make as little noise as possible. I reach to pull the vines back and the temperature on my hand drops 50 degrees.

What the……what is going on out here? Why is it so cold?

Cautiously, I step out of the cave. Looking around I see nothing but bright white fog in every direction. The arctic air makes me shiver and I realize I left my jacket inside the cave. I turn to go back but the cave is gone.

Yeah….that's not weird………. What's happening?………Wait. I must still be dreaming. That's it. I'm dreaming…..Okay….You can do this… Remember what you were taught about lucid dreaming………Control the dream….wake yourself……wake yourself.

I squeeze my eyes closed as hard as I can and open them.

I stand on a cliff now. Air hitting me in the face with intensity. Thunder rumbles above me causing my attention to be diverted to a large dark cloud with lighting swirling above my head. A bolt strikes the tree to my left, braking it in half. It tumbles to its death in the river below.

"Zaphora…..Zaphora……Zaphora…." A disturbing voice whispers in my ear.

I start to turn and feel a sharp pain in my shoulder. Blood drips down my back, down my side and into the patch of grass below me. I go to pull out the knife but someone beats me to it.

Relief and fear overcome me as blood gushes out of the wound at the absence of the knife.

The figure behind me is a lot larger than I am. Casting a shadow that blocks out the little sun that is in the sky. The artic temperature is numbing. So much so that I can no longer feel the blood oozing down my side.

I sigh in relief and feel three more sharp stabs piercing my back. One more in my right shoulder blade and two in my left.

Losing my balance, I fall forward and tumble towards the river.

I don't want to see, I can't bear to watch.

I close my eyes and feel the coolness of the water on my face.

I wake with a start and I'm back in the cave. My heart pounds out of my chest as I sit up on my bed of leaves. I blink a couple of times and realize that the sun is shining outside. It's morning. Even though I slept through the night, I feel more exhausted then I did before.

Where am I?.....Right....In a cave......on my spirit journey.......okay.....pull it together... you still have a long way to go.

I stable myself on my sore legs and began to gather my things. My stomach is still churning from the unsettling dream, so I decide to skip breakfast and start moving. Today is the day I meet with Shakira.

Chapter 4

I make my way north, taking only a few breaks to drink water from my canteen. The weight of last night's dream still heavy on my mind.

Instead of pacing myself, I take long strides to reach Shakira's hut. Driven by my desire to see if she can give me some guidance on such a traumatic vision.

My stomach starts to growl so I stop to pick some berries. I'm about to throw some in my mouth and stop myself, remembering my brother's words about his meeting with Shakira.

'She couldn't read my essence of lives past because she said that I was impure. Taking the repast of today into my essence before my reading, or something like that. She made me stay in her hut for 13 hours, until I was empty, before she could begin. What a waste of time.'

I put the berries in the pouch I had my strawberries in yesterday and place them in my bag. The last thing I need is to waste more time. I was already up after the sun, I refuse to lose any more hours of my spirit journey time hanging out at the hut of a sorceress. The berries can wait.

I wipe the perspiration from my brow as I approach Shakira's house. It is bigger than I expect it to be. Unlike the tent like structure made of sticks and leaves I had envisioned, it is quite a magnificent sight. Constructed of sculpted brick and stone with two huge windows that look upon me as I approach. A field of sunflowers about a mile long welcome me long before I reach the front door. I have only seen buildings like these in the books I have read, never in person.

She's doing better for herself than every member in my tribe, including my father, and he's the chief!

I lift my hand to knock and the door swings open.

"Come in my dear Zaphora, I have been expecting you." A voice echoes from inside of the house.

I step through the door taking in the surroundings. There are plants everywhere, engulfing my senses with their beautiful fragrances, as if I have stepped into a greenhouse. Hydrangeas, daisies, wildflowers, tulips all seem to follow me as I make my way through her house. I've never seen so many beautiful flowers in one place before.

"Keep walking my dear, I'm in the back." she says gently.

I make my way through a maze of flowers before I see a small brown-skinned woman with silver hair cutting a yellow daffodil off a tree. She also holds a pink gladiolus, a purple hyacinth, a purple lilac, a pink snapdragon, and what looks like a king protea.

"Take a seat my dear, I'll be right with you." She says, never looking back at me.

I walk over to a small wooden table in the middle of the room with two chairs on either side. A pot of tea, two cups, a candle, and a vase filled with water sit on top. I set my bag and bow on the floor and take a seat in one of the chairs.

Shakira turns slowly and makes her way over to me, almost hovering in her stride. As she gets closer I see she is a beautiful woman. Her skin radiates like that of a bronzed goddess. Her eyes, magnified due to the white rimmed glasses she wears, are hazel mysteries that almost fade into her skin. Her silver hair is secured in a loose bun at the top of her head, and seemed to glow, engulfing the room in light.

She places the flowers in the vase and begins to take off one petal from each flower. Lifting the top off the teapot, she places each petal inside. At the placement of the last petal, the pot puffs with smoke. She then pours 2 cups of tea, placing one in front of me.

"Drink, my dear Zaphora. We have much to discuss." she says, lifting her own cup and taking a sip.

I lift my cup and smell the tea. Not bad. It almost smells like chamomile. I place the cup on my lips and drink. The taste is bitter, like strained soggy grass. I feel ill as soon as it hits my stomach. The room gets hazy, the way the forest did that time I ate those bad mushrooms. My eyes flutter as I try to clear my vision. Shakira head seems to be larger than the rest of her body now. Protruding to my side of the table.

"Are……you……okaaaaaayyyyy…….my dear?…………" She says, but her voice sounds slowed. Delayed.

"What's going on?" I say, trying to lift my hands to my head but they feel like 100 pound weights.

"It's……okay……..my dear………just relax… "

I close my eyes and try to relax but my head is pounding. I open my eyes and Shakira is now behind me, her hands on my head. I look up and notice her eyes are closed and she is chanting something. I try to focus on the words, to see if I can catch what she is saying, but my hearing starts to leave me. A small echo remains, and then, nothing. I try to bring my hands to my ears to see what's blocking them but I can't move. A cold feeling creeps across my chest. I look down and see white shadow figures begin to escape from me. I'm overcome with a hollow feeling and I pass out.

Zaphora……….Open your eyes sweetie…………A soft voice whispers to me.

I open my eyes and I'm covered in armor standing in a field of grass and weeds. The stench of burning bushes fills my nostrils. The screams of the wounded warriors haunts the air around me.

"What are you doing? Pick up your sword and fight!" A man yells to me a few feet away, and then stabs another man in the chest. I watch the body hit the grass and blink out of my stupor.

At my feet is a tempered sword. The kind we use to read about in our lessons. I lift the sword and find that it's heavier than I thought it would be; but I quickly find my footing.

An angry, hefty solder charges toward me, axe in hand. He swings and I dodge his blow, counteracting with my own strike slicing through his gut. *What? How did I know how to do that?* The man falls to his death at my feet. I look back and see the man who warned me stab another man through the chest. He walks over to me and grabs my waist, engulfing me in a passionate kiss.

Cheers come from behind me. I break away from the kiss and turn to see what is going on.

A group of people dressed in all white are cheering and throwing rice at me.

"I love you honey." Says a man's voice to my left.

I look over and see a different handsome man in a tuxedo holding my arm and smiling at me. He leans over and gives me a kiss and it feels like I've known him my whole life. I notice that I am now in a long white dress with pointy shoes that hurt my feet. I smile back at him and we walk through the crowd hand and hand. *Is this what love feels like?*

We step through the double doors of the church and I am engulfed in darkness and alone. There is a single lit door with a long mirror attached to the front a few feet away. When I reach the door I notice I wear a black hemp shirt, a brown leather jacket and black leather pants. In the mirror a face I don't recognize stares back at me. There is a vertical stripe of black paint starting from my forehead and continuing to my chin. The sides of my head are shaved, leaving 5 long locks secured and hanging loosely from the top of my head. My eyes are the only thing that feels familiar. I can recognize that fear anywhere. I reach for the doorknob and it vanishes.

Okay........What now?

I slump next to the door trying to plot my next move. *There has got to be a way out of here.* The light above my head starts to flicker and then cuts off completely. It is so dark I can't see my legs in front of me. My right shoulder burns and I reach over to feel where the pain is coming from. Footsteps move quickly toward me and a hand reaches out of the darkness and pushes me through the mirror. I fall into a moving stream and swim to the nearest bank. Lifting my soaking body out of the water.

I look up and discover I am now at a burial ground. There is a funeral commencing a couple of feet from where I stand. Moving closer to the arrangement I realize that I know the people crying around a grave. They are my friends, my family, my tribe. Hesitantly, I creep closer to take a look into the casket. It is my father.

"What.......what is this?" I croak, my voice a little above a whisper.

"You! You did this to him! It's your fault." Sasha screams and points at me.

"What? What are you talking about?" I scream back.

But it's too late, they are already making their way over to me. Hate in their eyes. I walk backwards slowly. Shaking my head. Tears streaming down my cheeks. They start towards me in a slow jog. I turn and run as fast as I can.

What do they mean it's my fault? How can that be? I love my father, how am I responsible for his death?

My head pounds as my feet hit the ground with fury. I must get away from here. Away from this.

"Zaphora......Over here" Zeke yells at me through the trees.

"Zeke?" My direction changes and I make my way toward him. We run. Insults hit our backs. Branches smack our faces. I trip. Zeke picks me up and pulls me along. We hop a log and run around a hill, entering a small opening on the side. The tribe runs past us. Disappearing deeper into the woods.

Inside we catch our breaths and I can't believe what I'm seeing. Zeke peeks his head out the opening. Making sure the coast is clear.

Although he is older now, with facial hair and muscles than I remember, there is no mistaking him. My brother is alive!

"I think we got away." He says, turning to me.

"Zeke!" I say embracing him. "What are you doing here?"

"It's a long story Zaphora, and there is no time. Listen, I need to tell you something. Our father is not who you think he is… ...."

The setting begins to fade away like an old picture.

"Zeke! I can't here you ....wait! Don't go! What do you mean?" My vision gets blurry. I lose control of my body and hit the floor.

Darkness.

"Well, that was interesting." Shakira says, and leans over to blow out the candle. "Here dear, place this on your head." She hands me a white cloth that smells like honey and strawberries. I take the cloth and put it on my head and my headache subsides instantly.

"What ……what was that? Where was I? Why was my father dead? Why was Zeke there? What just happened?" I utter so fast that the words run into each other.

"Calm yourself Zaphora. I know you have many questions. And we have a lot to discuss. Please, come this way." She says and glides to the back of the room.

I stand and follow behind her, leaving the cloth on the table. She opens a small door that only someone her size can fit through and walks through. Ducking I walk in and close the door behind me.

"My child….my child. This day has plagued my dreams for some time now. I could never see a face though. But it was you." She says, turning towards me before continuing "Here I was thinking we were going to have a normal reading. Picking flowers, drinking tea and such, but boy was I wrong! Please excuse the mess my dear, I wasn't expecting company." She says, clearing some papers and books off her tiny couch. "Please have a seat; we have a lot of ground to cover."

Chapter 5

I pick up a small pillow and place it on my lap for comfort before taking a seat on the petite couch.

"Is there anything I can get you my dear? Something to eat or drink perhaps?" She says, fixing herself a cup of tea.

"Uh, no thank you. I don't think I need to pass out again." I say, looking at her skeptically.

She laughs "I understand your suspicion my dear, but what I did was necessary for me to get the information I need to help you on your journey. I have all of the information I need now, so if you would like a refreshment, I will be happy to provide that for you."

"Yes, that may be so, but a warning would have been nice. I thought I was dying." I say, shaking my head in disbelief. "I'm fine though, thank you for asking. What were those things coming from my chest before I passed out?"

"Those were..... how can I put this.....The spirits of your past lives. When I conduct a normal reading, the spirits of one's past lives help me to guide them in what they should be looking for during their journey. If you have ever heard the term that history repeats itself, that is usually also the case with a person's destiny."
She stops to stir some honey into her tea before continuing.
"9 times out of 10, if left unguided, a person is doomed to repeat the same mistakes of their past. It is my destiny to prevent that from happening. To guide the voyager in a way that they make better decisions in this life then they did in their last. This helps the voyager to eventually become what we know he or she can be. A leader. And so on and so forth until

our collective greatness brings our whole civilization to the next level of evolution."

"But that makes no since! In all the books I have read we have been taught that there are leaders and there are followers. Leaders are strong and pave the way for revolution and advancement. And followers are the backbone of the community; Giving the leader a reason to lead. People to lead. It's impossible to have a community where everyone is a leader. Then who would follow orders?" I say, noticeably irritated at the thought.

Shakira takes a long sip of her tea before responding. "See my dear Zaphora, that's where you have it wrong. You were taught about the leaders of the past to teach you what DIDN'T work. In every story you've ever read. In every example of your current life, or even your past lives for that matter, you have seen time and time again how one person's leadership over another ends in pain and strife. Humans have always had a hunger for power. Always believing that it is their destiny to lead their people to greatness. In actuality, we all have that responsibility, and the moment one person dims the shine of another, it not only affects the dimmed, but the dimmer."

"I don't understand."

"Let me put it to you this way Zaphora. There is room on this planet for us all to be great. Every one of us is a piece of a larger puzzle. We are all one soul. And when a piece of that larger soul is dimmed, we all suffer. To truly be what we as the human race were destined to be, we have to shed the ego and embrace the truth. We are all great. We are all leaders."

"Well, if we are all great, how come I am the only one who has ever had a reading like this? Why was I prophesized and no one else, not even my brother Zeke?" I say.

"Wow, quite the ego on you I see. I guess I shouldn't be surprised, considering your past lives and all. We'll have to work on that." She says, sitting next to me on the couch. "But for now, just know that your reading, like a lot of things you will experience in life, is just another tool to help you get to where you are supposed to be. My knowing more about your journey doesn't make you more important than those who've come before, and those who will come after you. It just means that I have been given the gift of giving you a bigger puzzle piece than you would have gotten on your own."

"What do you mean a bigger puzzle piece? What makes my reading so much different from the others you've done in the past?"

"Well, your reading not only allowed me to see the spirits of your past lives, but also the spirits of your future journey as well." She says, taking another sip of her tea.

"So how do you know which spirits are from my past and which are my future?" I ask confused.

"We'll start from the beginning, so try to keep up" She winks at me and continues "Your first past life was when you were battling in the burning field. You where the great Arab Queen Zenobia, and the man that was fighting alongside you was your husband. In the 3rd century you and your husband expanded your territory into Palestine, Syria, Egypt and Lebanon before you were captured. Your second past life was a little vaguer though. Based on the feelings that you were transmitting I could feel that the man that was standing by your side was your husband as well, in a more modern since of course. But what really boggles my brain is the energy that I received from both men. That through all lives your essence was connected to his for eternity. What I can't grasp though is how. Never in my 120 years of doing this have I encountered a person whose essence was eternally linked to another's. You two, in every sine of the word, are soul mates."

"So does that mean that we will be linked in this life as well? That the person I am meant to live the rest of my life with has already been chosen for me?"

"No not necessarily. The soul is more complex than most human minds can understand. Linked souls are not always based in romance. They come in all forms. A mother and daughter. Uncle and niece. Cousins. But the ones mostly written about is that of husband and wife. So you see my dear Zaphora, you may marry whomever you choose. Cultivate whatever relationships you choose. Because weather you know it or not, your soul mate will find their way to you, if they haven't already."

"Well that makes me feel a little better. Knowing that I have some sort of say over the life I choose to lead."

"You have all the say. I am only hear to give you information. All decisions are up to you. You are the master of your own destiny and you can do what you will with the information given." She says, finishing off her tea and placing it on the rustic wooden table next to her.

"What about……..the funeral? And……and Zeke?" I ask, hesitantly, not really wanting to know the answer.

"I'm sad to say my dear that the funeral and your meeting with your brother has yet to happen." She says, looking down at her small feet.

"So what you're saying is that it will happen? That my father will die and Zeke is still alive!" I say, almost screaming.

"Well, it's a little more complicated than that. The events that will happen may unfold a little differently than you've just experienced based on the choices you make. But it is true however that the substance of each situation remains the same. Your father will die. And you will meet back up with your brother" She says, almost folding into herself.

The air leaves my lungs and refuses to re-enter. Black spots begin to cloud my vision. My heart pounds in my ears and gives me an instant migraine. Water wells in my eyes and I let out a moan. The weight of it all is too much to bear and I break. Sobbing uncontrollably in my hands.

So many questions. Too much information. My father. My brother. I can't take it. I can't breathe.

I feel a small hand on my back.

"I know it is a lot to swallow my dear. Here, take this, it will help with your head." She says, handing me a purple drink with a eucalyptus leaf floating at the top. I take the drink from her and sip it slowly, the lavender flavor goes down smoothly. After a couple of minutes my head doesn't hurt as much.

"I......I don't understand." I utter, after regaining some air. "Why am I seeing all of this? Why is this happening to me?"

"I wish I could tell you my dear but I don't know. What I can tell you is that the answers you seek are in the east. That's where the next part of your journey unfolds." She says, her hand still rubbing my back.

"What if I don't want to continue? What if I just go home and barricade myself in my room for the rest of my life? Then those things won't happen! Then none of what I saw will come true!" I say with as much confidence as I can muster.

"I wish it was that easy my dear, but it is not. The events will happen with or without your participation. The only choice you have in the matter is if you will take part in your history, and become the person you were meant to be, or if you will die an old lady locked in her parents' house wandering *what if?*" She stops rubbing my back and sits on the couch to look into my eyes. "And something tells me you are not the type of person to just sit back and do nothing." she says with a grin.

She was right. I was not raised to watch time pass by without making my mark in it. Even though the knowledge that my father will pass away soon was scary. What's more frightening is waiting for the inevitable and not doing anything about it.

I wipe my tears with the back of my hand and try to focus my thoughts.

"I did have some other questions for you, not related to the reading. That's if you have some spare time to help me?" I say looking back at her.

"I will do all I can to help you my dear Zaphora. What would you like to know?"

"Yesterday, when I was in the forest looking for shelter for the night, I thought I saw a black figure in a cloud of smoke. As soon as I noticed it, the figure fled and the smoke disappeared. That same night I had a dream about that same figure. I just wanted to know if you think that it means anything, or if I was hallucinating the whole thing?"

"If you hadn't just started your spirit journey yesterday, I might think that you were hallucinating. But taking into consideration the reading we just had, I would say that you did in fact see what you thought you saw." She takes a pause before answering. As if trying to gather the right words to tell me what I saw. "A figure in smoke or fog is usually someone projecting a spirit. But a dark figure…..that also appears in your dreams……" She pauses. "That means that the figure following you is a dark one with a lot of power in sorcery and magic. These figures are unable to harm you in reality, but can do so in your dreams. What else was in this dream that you had?" She asks, intrigued.

"The dark figure touched my face and caused this black liquid to cover my body. I couldn't move or look away, all I could do was wait to be swallowed whole……….But………I do remember…. right before I couldn't see anymore, the figure's head tilted slightly. I don't know, like it felt sorry for me or something."

"Felt sorry for you? That IS very curious." she says rubbing her chin. "The only other time I've heard of that happening …." She stands and heads over to a bookshelf in the corner. Running her fingers through the titles, she grabs one titled "Dark Forces of Magic". Skimming through the pages she stops for a minute and reads. "Here it is! Yes, just as I thought. If what you thought you saw was remorse, it says here that the dark figure has some sort of connection to you, through blood." She slowly looks up at me.

"Through blood!" I exclaim. "So whatever is stalking me is. ....related to me?"

"That's what it looks like. Who do you think would want to hurt you that you are related to? Mother? Father? Cousin? Your brother perhaps?" She says, looking at me over her glasses.

"No, none of those people. I can't think of anyone. My family and I are very close. We love each other and would do anything for one another." I scream, shaking my head.

"Okay, if you say so........I'm just the messenger." She says, closing the book and placing it back on the shelf. "So did you have any other questions for me my dear?"

I think hard and remember the second part of my dream.

"Yes, I do!" I start. But pause briefly, trying to describe that part of the dream. "Ummm, there was a bigger shadowy figure in my second dream. It hovered over me and stabbed me in the back several times. I was on a cliff so the final stab sent me over the edge. Do you think that means anything?"

"Well......there's not much to go on with that dream. I can tell you that the knife in the back is symbolic that someone will betray you multiple times. I can't however tell you who that person is and why they will do so. Where you able to see anything about the hovering figure? Anything that sticks out to you as being odd?"

"Nothing about the figure......but before I knew he was behind me, there was a storm cloud above me and the lightning from it struck a branch next to me which broke and fell into the river. That was kind of odd."

"That's good. You are very perceptive my dear. That means that before you are betrayed, you will be warned first, and better prepared to handle the situation better. Pay attention to the signs the earth gives you. They will never lead you wrong." She says, kissing me on the forehead.

Chapter 6

It takes me a while to get my barring's about me so Shakira lets me stay overnight. The floor is hard and uncomfortable but at least it's warm. It took 3 of her little blankets to cover my 6 foot frame but I was grateful for her hospitality.

I rose before the sun to get a start on the day, and to my surprise she had already awoke. I folded her throws and placed them neatly on her couch before picking up my bag and bow and making my way to the door. Shakira stands in the Spirit Reading Room picking flowers, for her upcoming reading I assume.

"Thank you Shakira. For everything. You've really been very kind." I say with a gracious smile.

"It was the least I could do after telling you that your world was falling apart." she giggles a little to herself.

"Whelp, I know you have to be on your way so I made you some breakfast to go. It's wrapped in that napkin over there on the table." She head gestures to the table in the middle of the room. "See to it that you put something on your stomach before you walk too much and pass out. You're no good to anyone that way. "

"Thank you. You didn't have to........Thank you!" I say as I pick up the food and head for the exit.

"Your welcome my dear. Good luck to you and your Journey, may you find the answers you seek." she says, and turns back to her plants.

I leave Shakira's hut and head east like she instructed. About a mile down the road I remember the breakfast in my bag. In the napkin she's placed 4 blueberry muffins and 2 hardboiled eggs. I eat the eggs first and finish with the muffins right as the sun rises. When I'm done I feel lighter on my feet and more energetic.

I guess I was hungry.

Half the day has past and I am still walking east. Not knowing who or what I am looking for. I decide to stop just before crossing the stream to rest and meditate for direction. Whatever it is I am supposed to be looking for probably isn't going to find me today. My stomach growls a little as I take a seat on a rock and put my feet in the water. I take out the berries I picked before I went to Shakira's house and pop a couple in my mouth, along with some ham my mother packed for me and take a big gulp of water.
Crossing my legs and steadying myself on the rock, I close my eyes and begin my meditation. The crisp air fills my lungs and instantly embraces me with a warm calmness. I'm deep into my meditation when I hear rustling in the trees behind me. I turn quickly and see nothing in either direction. *You're hearing things again Zaphora!* I look up at the sky, shaking my head at my paranoia. Taking a moment to admire the beautiful eagle flying above me. The sun warms my face and I close my eyes and take it all in. The trees rustle again. A branch falls from one of the trees above me and hits the water. I put my finger up to check the wind. There is none. The brand on my arm begins to sting and I get a feeling in the pit of my stomach. *Something's Off.*

Pressure in my back sends me flying into the stream before me. I splash around a moment before regaining my focus. Once I get centered I look back to where I was pushed and see two little boys are running away with my bags.

Climbing out of the stream I feel a sudden twinge of déjà vu. It's beginning.

As quickly as my legs can manage I immediately begin chase. They are much faster than the little boys in my tribe; and they have a head start so their advantage is evident. I need to find another way to increase my odds. Barefoot, darting and dashing through trees and rocks along the way; I look up as I run and see the branches are thick enough to climb. I leap to the tree in front of me and climb up the side. They are about a mile down the path now. Springing from tree to tree I make chase. Two more trees and I will be directly over one of them, and the other will have to stop.

Mounting myself at the end of the second trees' branch I pounce on the chubby short haired boy lagging behind.

"Ahhhhhhhhh!" he screams in pain as I turn him over.

"What is wrong with you! Didn't your guardians teach you that you aren't supposed to take things that don't belong to you?" I growl into his face, breathing heavily with each word.

"You....You're hurting me..." He wines. With tears streaming from his eyes he glares at the arm I'm pinning to the ground. I follow his gaze and see that my nails are longer than I remember them being and that they are piercing his skin, causing the dirt below him to become red with blood. I release him in shock and stumble backwards.

The other boy has stopped in his tracks. He stands with his mouth open staring at me in shock and fear. My bag rests at his feet.

"I......I'm so sorry, I didn't mean......I'm sorry." I say, shaking my head.

"Come on man, let's get outta here! This lady is crazy!" The short chubby boy says as he runs towards the tall lanky one, who is still staring at me in horror. The chubby boy finally pulls the tall one and breaks his gaze and they take off down the path.

I cringe at the sight of blood on my hands and walk over to the stream to wash them off. My reflection is off slightly. A little darker than I remember it being. And my eyes........I take a closer look in the water and notice my eyes are crystal blue with black centers......*What is happening to me?*.........I open my eyes a little more with my hands and notice my nails are back to how I remember them. I look back in the stream and my eyes are mocha brown again. The stinging of my brand begins to subside but I feel a small sting on my left shoulder blade.

What was that? What is going on with me?????

Picking up my bags I cross the stream and continue to head east. I'm so engulfed in my thoughts that when I look up the sun has set and I'm still walking east.

The people of the old world dropped so many bombs during their war that they blanketed the sky many years ago, causing the stars to barely shine through the thick fog and making it almost impossible to see two feet in front of me. It is time to call it a night.

Rite of Passage / New Earth Series Volume I / 48

I reach in my bag and pull out the torch I made the night before to help me navigate the woods. After walking for a couple of miles with no caves in sight, I decide to sleep next to a large rock a couple of feet away. I'm about to extinguish the torch when a howling wolf makes me second guess my sleeping arrangements. The trees above me look steady enough to hold my weight for the night so I find a sturdy one and begin to climb. I'm about 5 feet from the ground when I adjust myself on a branch and secure my bag above me. My hood goes over my nearly frozen ears and I close my eyes and try to rest.

The wind is icy on my face and I feel as the presence of someone standing over me. I open my eyes and my surroundings are in black and white, like a picture from earlier generations. The fog begins to grow in the trees to my right. As my eyes begin to focus I see the dark figure emerging and moving in my direction. I reach for my bow but it's gone, along with my bags. Stumbling to my feet I run as fast as I can in the opposite direction. Nothing but fog and trees stretch in every direction. I stop and rest near a tree and turn to see if the figure is still behind me. A net snaps off the ground, trapping me in a hovering apparatus. Dangling upside down, I can see the figure is only a couple of feet from me now, and there is nowhere to run. The figure reaches for me and I close my eyes, awaiting the inevitable.

*Zaphora.......I'm coming for you.........*The voice, raspy and deep, whispers in my ear, causing it to heat instantly. I shudder and open my eyes and it is daylight.

The sun warms my cheeks and makes it hard to see. As my vision clears I realize that I am far from where I was when I fell asleep. I am in some box made of sticks and twine riding in what seems like a horse drawn wagon. There's a man, who looks like he is wearing a hooded woven sack for a coat, driving the wagon. My bags and bow and arrow sit beside him. Frantically, I search for a way out of this box. I reach for the lock on the top and a shock goes through my body.

"Ahhh" I scream, trying to move around "What is going on....Where are you taking me?" I shout.

"She's up!" A high pitch voice says. "I wouldn't touch that if I where you" A deep voice says "That lock isn't going to open for anyone but me."

"What do you mean? Where are you taking me? Let me out of here!" I demand.

'Well you're a feisty one." the deep voice says. "And not very nice," the pitchy voice says "not at all like the lady I thought you would be."

"Well if you must know, that lock back there is enchanted, so you might as well get comfortable because you're not getting out of there for a while. We still have a whole day's ride ahead of us and it won't do any of us any good if you keep running your mouth like a pesky little bird." The deep voice says.

I sit looking at the man talking to me and realize that from where I sit there is only one hooded man controlling this wagon, so where is the other voice coming from?

How did he sneak up on me? Who is he? Where is he taking me?

"Look. I don't know who you are or why you felt the need to kidnap me while I was asleep but I really don't have time for this right now. I have a journey to finish and a lot of questions that need to be answered. So if you would kindly let me out of this contraption I will gladly be on my way and you won't have to worry about my pesky bird voice any longer." I state, confidently, staring at the back of his cloak.

"Oh no my dear. It won't be that easy to get rid of me." says the pitchy voice.

 "I know someone who would pay top Shin for a girl such as yourself. So how about I do us both a favor and cut this conversation short." The deep voice says as he reaches for a burgundy blanket. Turning, he throws the blanket over my box.

My lids feel heavy instantly. I try to fight it but my eyes close and I fall asleep.

Chapter 7

Leaves fall on my head as an eagle flies off the branch above me, jerking me awake. As I regain my consciousness, I notice that the sun is setting and that I am tied to a tree with my hands behind me. I struggle and try to free myself but stop when I realize that I am only cutting my skin on the bark.

"Ah, struggling is futile my dear. You're not going anywhere until I'm ready for you to." The deep voice says behind me. He walks around the tree I see the bottom half of his scarred face under the hood of his tattered coat. With the flick of his wrist the rope tightens more around me.

"Owwww! What do you want from me?" I scream, holding back the tears welling in my throat.

"Members of your tribe are a hot commodity here in The Dunes. And you're going to be my ticket out this hell hole!" He says, grinning to show a sharpened row of yellow teeth.

Terrified, I look around and see nothing but sand and hills in either direction. My lion on my arm burns so bad it feels like it just might burst into flames.

What do I do? Think Zaphora! Think!

"Ahh, here he comes." The high-pitched voice says, looking at a truck driving up one of the hills.

But I notice that his mouth doesn't move. How is that possible?

The truck pulls next to the wagon and a pale thin man with red hair hops out of the driver seat, pulling a black bag out of the back seat before heading over in our direction. A few feet away from his truck he separates into two people. I blink twice not quite believing what I just saw.

"Don't you hate it when he does that? I hate it when he does that." The hooded man says looking back at me.

"Leave it up to Sharif to meet all the way out here in the middle of nowhere. Man I swear you're one of the most paranoid people I know!" One of the red haired men says as he gets closer. The other one reaches into the black bag and pulls out a dead iguana and tosses the iguana to Sharif. "I brought you a little snack. I figured you had been waiting here for a while."

Sharif catches the iguana and opens the top button of his cloak to reveal another mouth. He ravishes the iguana as if he hasn't eaten for days.

"We like, we like!" the pitchy voice says from the second mouth as he stuffs the last leg into his mouth.

What the heck are these things? I didn't know there were people who lived outside of the Greenlands. Well besides Shakira and the Silliloquii tribe. The Silliloquii tribe……..Is this what they've become?

The red hared men circle the tree like vultures circling their pray. Their thinning hair moves stiffly in the windy desert, showing pieces of their scalps. Taking in every inch of me. My stomach turns in disgust.

"Ohhhhh" one says, looking at my legs. "This is a strong one. Look how toned her muscles are." the other one says, finishing his sentence.

"And look" Sharif says peeling back my bandage, "Her brand is fresh, maybe a couple of days old. That means she's only just hit her 18th year!"

"Yes Sharif, you did good old friend." The red haired men say, rubbing their hands together in unison "Here is your payment, as promised. The goods are exactly as you say they are." The red haired man tosses Sharif a black bag. "I guess this is the last time I'll see you around these parts. What will you do with your new found fortune?"

"Eh, I don't know. Find me a nice spot by the ocean somewhere. Some good grub and a couple of ladies. Maybe retire you know? I've been living this life for a long time. I'm looking forward to living the rest of my days living off the fat of the land."

"Sounds good man!" The other red haired man says "You deserve it! What are you like 100 now?"

"140 actually. And I can still catch the big fish!" Sharif says a matter-of-factly.

What! 140???? People don't live past 100. At least that's what my father always told me. This defies his logic. Why would he lie to me? Maybe he doesn't know. Maybe Sharif's not a person at all. He does have that creepy second mouth. This is all way too much for me to wrap my head around.

"Well," says Sharif, tossing the bag over his shoulder "I'll be on my way now. It was nice doing business with you for all these years. You take care of yourself." he turns and heads back to his wagon.

"You too old man. Try to stay out of trouble." One of the red heads yell after him.

"I can't make any promises." Sharif says, hoping on his wagon. And then he is gone, leaving behind only a cloud of dust.

"Well, I guess it's about time I get you back to HQ." the red head on my right says.

"And get my long awaited promotion" the red head on my left says.

"And don't try no funny business either!" he says leaning in so close that I can smell the fish on his breath "I can easily bring back your dead body and get what I need out of this deal."

I swallow hard and decide to keep my comments to myself, before my smart mouth gets me killed.

Chapter 8

We arrive at HQ shortly after sundown. From a distance it looks like more sand, stretched in all directions. But as we get closer I see a slight ruffle in the sky, like I'm looking through a glass of water. We stop shortly before the ruffle and man camouflaged in a sand cloak looks in the truck and waves us by. The sand opens to a tunnel a couple of feet away, and we drop beneath the earth. We drive past a guard post at the entrance of the cave, then through a long tunnel, and a whole underground city appears before my eyes.

The music hits my ears before we exit the tunnel. It is so loud and echoed that the words the woman is singing are almost inaudible. The red haired man and his clone ride slowly in silence down the dusty path, stopping every so often to let a running child pass. Neon signs and electric generated lanterns light our path as we descend deeper into the cave. People are everywhere I turn; loud talking, dancing and groping each other. The stench is a cross between garbage and roasted deer, making my stomach do flips with every bump in the road.

After what seems like miles we come to a stop in front of a huge, abandoned looking building. The clones pull me out of the back of the truck and escort me toward the double doors.

Two huge men guard the doors as we approach. They acknowledge the red haired men with a head nod and open the doors.

"Hey Jax! Skits is in The Dome. He's expecting you." one of the toned men says before closing the door behind us.

Inside, the musty aroma is overwhelming. The hallway is dimly lit and narrow, causing the red haired clone to meld his self into one man again. I'm not sure if it's my nervousness, or being cooped up in this humid, narrowing hallway, but I start to sweat profusely.

We make a right, exiting the hallway, and almost run into an intoxicated woman. She burps in my face and laughs as if it was the funniest thing she's seen all day. Jax pulls me past her and we make our way through the hordes of people ahead. Some are yelling at loud, blinking machines. Others are standing around tables with plastic androids in front of them shouting at each other.

I thought these objects were forbidden. Why is everyone here freely using them out in the open?

We pass a room where people are standing with various animals in cages next to them. They are all yelling and watching a chicken and duck fight in the center.

In another room there are men and women in cages. I take a closer look and see that they all have some sort of deformity. Some have horse bottoms. Two are in a tank with fins and gills. One woman has horns. Another man has the face of a pig.

"What is this place?" I say under my breath.

"Pretty couce right?" Jax says, grinning at me.

"What? What is couce?" I say, confused.

"You tribees. So stuck in your little boxes. It means cool, awesome, amazing….."

"Oh" I say "I guess that's one word for it."

Rite of Passage / New Earth Series Volume I / 57

A man who looks part cow notices me staring at him and gives me a scolding look, followed me a loud "Mooooo". I quickly look away and make a mental note not to stare at anyone here for longer than a couple of seconds.

We get on an elevator and a bald stocky man who is no taller than my waist stands next to the numbers. He looks at me then over at the red haired man, shakes his head and presses the big black button marked "DOME".

We go down 50 floors before the doors open. A tall gate a couple of feet away is all that separates me from what looks like a large ring in the center of an arena. I'm pushed through the gate and my face hits the blood spattered sand. My restraints are cut and some sort of device is placed on my ankle. I jump to my feet and turn to see Jax grinning at me from the other side of the gate. I watch him until he disappears into the darkness. The bleeding sand refocuses my attention and I wonder how many people have died in here?

A curvy lady with a headset sashays over to me with a dagger in her hand, blade in. As she gets closer, I notice she has a long brown tail sticking out the back of her pants that's few shades darker than her skin. She then rips the bandage off my brand and tosses the blade into the sand next to my head and smirks in amusement. I don't know what it is about her but my stomach boils in hatred for this woman. Her eyes are pure evil, and she needs to be put down like that wolf in the forest. She must see the fury in my eyes at her smugness because she backs away onto a platform that levitates her to the center of the ring before speaking.

"Ladies, Gentlemen and Beautiful Creatures" She starts "Welcome to The Dome's much anticipated finally!"

The crowd goes wild with cheers and fist pumps. I take the blade and begin to cut the rope holding my hands together. The blade is pretty sharp so it cuts the rope with ease. I look over to the lady with the tail and try to think of a way to knock her off her pedestal when I spot Jax taking a bag from a chubby man with a funny fur hat on sitting on some kind of throne behind her.

What is this….some sort of battle? Have I been brought and sold 2 times today just to die in this ring?

"I am your host, Sitrine" she says, interrupting my thought "Thank you all for coming out tonight. Your generous contributions are appreciated. In this corner we have Santee, our competitor from the meek tribe of Janti…… "She says pointing at a thin, pale girl with stark white hair cowering in the corner.

"Aww, look at those eyes. She's frightened. It's okay sweetie, it will all be over soon, and on the bright side, you might meet one of your relatives crossing over." she pauses to let the crowd react. They laugh loud and hard, some fall out of their seats onto the floor.

"And in this corner we have Von, our challenger from the all-knowing, all-seeing Xouxi tribe." she points at a tall, dark, muscular man who looks around with confusion in his eyes.

"I bet you didn't see this coming though did you?" she laughs, and the crowd joins along.

"In this corner we have our champion, and house favorite, from the tribe of Sililoquii…."

Rhuh...Rhuh....Rhuh.... The crowd chants, fist pumping into the air.

"The muscular, the ruthless, the handsome and talented ....Santoooooooooos!" she says, lifting her voice and octave and clapping her hands to emphasize that she too is a fan.

His eyes are merciless as he stares down Von from across the ring. He closes his eyes for a moment and moves his head from side to side, cracking his neck, and moving his wild, coal black main over his shoulders. The tribal markings that cover his arms and back, and deep wound that crosses his right eye only intensifies his intimidation.

How many times has he done this to be a crowd favorite?

The crowd erupts in cheers and chants. Spitting and yelling in delight. After about a minute they die down and she continues.

"And tonight will be a special treat for many of you. We bring to you, all the way from the Greenlands, and the mysterious tribe of Seraphine..." she covers the microphone and looks over at me "What's your name dear?"

I stare back at her in disgust. Why would I willingly participate in this bloodbath? What....Do I look danger deprived or something? I've had enough bizarre events happen to me in the past 3 days to last a lifetime, so she's crazy if she thinks I will just go along with all of this craziness.

She rolls her eyes, looks past me and nods. A shock is sent up my leg from the device I forgot Jax put on my before leaving me in this ring. I lose all control of my leg and go crashing to the floor, feeling paralyzed.

"We can do this all day honey" she says "Or you can tell me your name so I can get this show on the road."

"Z…..Zzzzaphora" I push out through gritted teeth.

"Zaphora from the Seraphine tribe everyone." she says with contempt, cutting her eyes at me.

The crowd bursts into ohhs and aahs. They all look at me like I'm some sort of magical creature, when to me, they are the ones that are abnormal. I gain movement back in my body and lunge for the dagger a couple of feet from me and prepare to fight.

It's going to be a long night.

Chapter 9

"The rules are simple. Women fight women, and men fight men. Anything goes. You don't leave the ring until one of you is unable to continue. Unconscious or otherwise." she says, looking over at me. A chill goes down my spine. The crowd sounds like a muffled speaker and I'm finding it hard to breath. I can't take a life! But I can't very well let her take my life either.

Santee and I catch eyes for a moment and I see something primal in her. Her stance is that of a fighter now, a lot different from the meek demeanor she displayed at the beginning of the introductions. She holds a samurai sword with a red handle in the stance of a warrior. I wince at the thought of that blade cutting through my flesh, ending my life.

Von holds a spear like weapon. The wooden handle sits ready to attack in his left hand, the seven spiked tips reflect the light as he tries his best to suppress his nervousness.

Santos holds two hand-held axes for weapons with sharp edges on one end and spiked edges on the other. He sways back and forth in his corner, sizing up his opponent. His energy could make even the fiercest lion run for cover. I am suddenly relieved I'm not Von.

And then there's me. With this tiny dagger and no experience whatsoever in killing a human being. Maybe I should have been nicer to Sitrine, so I could've at least gotten a better weapon.

The platform Sitrine stands on hovers over to the man with the funny fur hat and she steps off and sits next to him.

"Ready. Begin!" she says into the headset.

Santee and I circle each other in the right side of the ring.

We both stop for a moment to watch Santos approach Von. Spinning his axes around his hands as he gets closer. Von backs up slowly until he hits the edge of the gate. He takes a deep breath and charges at Santos with all of his might. Santos dodges his strike and kicks him in his rear. The crowd laughs as Von falls on his face.

My brand begins to burn.

I look back at Santee and notice she is making her way toward me with her sword elevated. She swings and I duck, but not before she slices my cheek with her blade. I wipe the blood from the cut before it can fall and run at her, sliding on my knees I cut her Achilles tendon with the dagger. She shrieks as a pool of blood covers her bare foot and falls to the floor.

The crowd ohhs and ahhs at the sight of blood in the ring.

"We've got a bleeder folks. You know what that means........." Sitrine says.

"CHRONOS! CHRONOS! CHRONOS!" chants the crowd.

"That's right! It's Chronos time!" she says in a saucy melody.

The ring begins to shake and rotate, throwing us all off balance, until a loud horn goes off. The floor stops moving and a cage begins to rise from a platform in the center of the ring. As it gets closer to the top I see 5 huge monkeys with horns holding two-handed claymores.

"CHRONOS! CHRONOS! CHRONOS!"

"Now we can't very well have the challenger that spilled the first blood fight the Chronos with just a dagger now can we?" says Sitrine.

"Nooooooo." The crowd says in unison.

A feeling of relief overcomes me, and all I can think is, please be a bow and arrow!

A hooded man walks out of a door behind me and hands me two weapons that look like fist boomerangs with blades.

"How do I even use these?" I say, looking at the weapons in confusion.

"Figure it out, or die, your choice." The clocked man says, shoving them at me and descends back to the door.

I place the dagger in my back pocket and try to get a grip on the new weapons. The cage door drops and the monkeys run out yelling and swinging their swords. One comes straight for me, swinging his sword wildly, cutting my arm. The sting catches me off guard and I stumble a bit. The monkey screams and ponds his chest with one fist. He looks back at me and charges again.

I'm ready this time. My feet to the floor. Watching the monkey's actions like I would if I were hunting. Trying to predict his next move, his next strike. He swings the blade, helicopter style, over his head and focuses on my neck as he approaches. Before he can swing, I fall to one knee, cross my arms over my chest and slice him through his gut. He drops his sword and grabs his stomach. An axe collides with his skull, splattering blood on my face. He looks at me with his wide, creepy eyes and falls to the ground. I look up where the monkey was standing to see Santos standing over me with an axe in his hand. He winks at me and goes after Von.

I look around for Santee and see her laid out in the corner, two monkeys standing over her eating her stomach. Her eyes empty, staring at me. I gag at the sight and turn away. On the other side of the arena I see Santos slit Von's throat. A siren goes off and the monkeys drop their weapons and make their way to the cages, dragging Von and Santee behind them.

"We have our winners!" Sitrine says, standing near the railing, glaring down at us. "Santoooooooosssssss!!!! And, what was her name again?" she says looking back at the crowd. "Oh yeah, and Zephra." she says, smirking at me.

Chapter 10

Santos makes his way over to me and pulls me into the center of the stadium, causing my shocked body to warm with his touch. He lifts one of my arms and the crowd cheers, throwing bread and cheese into the arena. He brakes his hold on my arm and starts collecting the bread and cheese.

"Don't just stand there looking stupid, pick something up." he says.

I start picking up some bread and cheese and 10 hooded men with long black sticks come out and surround us. Santos looks up, grabs one more piece of bread, and heads to the center of the ring. I follow suit, not knowing what to expect next. Once we are in the center the hooded men stop walking and a cage drops around us. We begin to descend into the floor, deeper and deeper until we can no longer hear the chants of the crowd. The deeper we go the darker it becomes. There are a few lanterns here and there but not nearly enough for me to see Santos standing a few feet from me.

"Where are we? Where are they taking us?" I utter.

"We're in The Dunes. They are taking us to our cells." he says in an irritated tone.

"Why are they making us fight each other? Who are these people? Is this what the Sililoquii tribe has become?"

"This is NOT the Sililoquii tribe. My people are resilient, not savages!" Santos yells in my direction. "Enough questions, I'm tired, and you're whining like a naive child." he snaps.

I swallow hard and hold all my other thoughts on my tongue. The last thing I meant to do was piss off the one person willing to talk to me about this place. And how did he get here? Was he taken like I was on his spirit journey as well? No that can't be right. The Silliloquii don't go on spirit journeys. So why is he...

The cage jolts as it reaches the bottom floor, knocking me off balance and train of thought. A small door opens and Santos steps in front of me to a bared cell made of concrete and steel a few feet away. A hooded man follows behind him and locks him in the room.

"We have a new champion." A deep voice says in the shadows.

"Not a very pretty one." Sitrine utters.

As they get closer the dim lit cave highlights Sitrine walking alongside the short bald man who I now realize was the man sitting on the throne in the arena. Santos looks over at us briefly and then continues to count the cheese and bread he's gathered.

"I guess Jax was right. You Seraphine women ARE more than meets the eye." the bald man says looking me up and down.

"Don't give this little girl more credit than she deserves." she snarls "she would have been Chronos food had it not been for Santos." she winks back at Santos, he looks up briefly and grins back then goes back to what he was doing.

"Nevertheless I think she is owed some congratulations for such a feat. Oh where are my manners. My name is Skits, I'm what you would call the owner of this humble establishment. It is a pleasure to make your acquaintance Zaphora." he kisses my hand and I almost gag.

I can't tell which one is more grotesque, his burnt skin and rotting teeth or the smell that emits from him every time he talks.

He is still holding my hand as he walks me to my cage in the wall. I try not to look at him or feel his rough skin grazing mine.

"I look forward to seeing more of you and what you have to offer." he says, closing the cell behind me.

I stand speechless staring at his deformed body as he glares at me.

"Let's go honey" Sitrine says, looping her arm with his "Dinner awaits!" She gives me one last icy look and heads down the corridor with Skits.

The pain hits me all at once as soon as they leave my sight. I place the bread and cheese I was able to gather in a small cooler at the end of my bed and touch the wound on my arm. Surprisingly, most of the blood is dried but has stained my pants and shirt pretty bad. A sliver of light hits a glass under the bed and I bend down to see a jar of leaching maggots. Those will work wonders for this wound on my arm.

I pick up a cloth off the tiny sink in the corner of the room and begin cleaning my wound. My body aches all over and I just want to sleep but I have to make sure this doesn't get infected.

Once the wound is as clean as I can get it I re-wet the cloth and clean some of the monkey's blood off of my face. Forgetting about the goodbye present Santee left to remember her by. I carefully clean the cut and realize that it's deeper than I originally thought. Great, it's going to leave a scar. I place the cloth back on the sink and sit on the edge of the cot, reaching to pick up the jar under it. About 5 green glowing maggots crawl on top and around each other in the jar. Reluctantly I open the lid and reach in to pull one out, slowly placing it on my wounded arm. The maggot conforms to the cut, stretching its body to cover every inch of the scar. Once it settles itself, I feel a cooling sensation shoot through my arm and the maggot glows lime green. I then lift the jar and look for the smallest one left and place that one over the scar on my face before putting the top back on and placing it under my bed.

Trying to get my mind off of the cool sensation coursing through my body, I lay on the cot and close my eyes. Images of my mother and father flood my thoughts. I miss them so much. How did I get here? I think, wiping the tears from my eyes. I can hear my father now. *'Pay attention to your surroundings Zaphora! Here you are the predator, but out there you are the prey'*. I never knew how right he was.

Chapter 11

Sleep comes eventually, but with much protest. A part of me will never sleep the same again after being snatched from that tree and brought to this hell. But the little bit of sleep the sandman did grant me came with a strange dream:

My eyes open and a beautiful woman sings an enchanting melody over me. There are wooden bars entrapping me in what looks like a crib of some sort. White, glowing butterflies circle the singing lady's head as she looks down at me. Her eyes safe and welcoming. Her skin is like fresh poured honey that has been sprinkled with glitter. She reaches for my face with her long fingers and I put my hands up to block hers. My arms are shorter than they should be and my hands are the size of baby oranges.

I close my eyes hard and open them again.

The sounds of shouting down the hall and a hoard of boots scuffing the floors welcome me back to reality. I sit up quickly on my cot and try to remember where I am. Spirit Journey. Woods. Truck. The Dunes. A tall, broad shouldered woman approaches my cell and looks over at me.

"Be ready in 10 minutes." she says sternly and walks off. "Oh, and make sure you eat something newbie, it's going to be a long day."

I remember the bread and cheese I put in the cooler at the end of my cot yesterday and reach in to eat some. My stomach growls to life with the first piece of bread I shove into my mouth and I realize I haven't really eaten in days. I start to devour the goods but slow down when the reality that I might not get any more food for a while hits me. I take a quick inventory of what I have left. 8 loafs of bread. 4 hunks of cheese. Then I make my way to the sink to drink some water.

"Two minutes!" a deep voice echoes in the hallway.

I look in the mirror and see that the maggots have stopped glowing. I carefully pull the deflated bug off my arm and face, making sure I don't leave any of its limbs attached to my skin. I throw the bugs in the sink, washing them down the drain. With my last minute I splash some water on my face in hopes that it will give me some energy. It doesn't.

"Stand against the wall newbie" The guard says, now back outside my cell.

I do as she says and she unlocks the cell, putting two magnetic cuffs on my wrists. The added weight reminds my arms of the long days I've had. She takes me down the hall where more guards and prisoners are walking in a row in front of me. We walk for through a maze of corridors until we reach two big steel doors with a "T" engraved in them. Two buff guards stand on each side of the doors opening them in unison to reveal a large grassy area filled with trees and a small lake. I look around in amazement that something this beautiful is so far underground.

The guards make us stand side by side until we are all in a circle in the middle of the grass field. We stand there as the guards begin walk in uniform fashion out of the steel doors. A short, harry man tries to run for the doors and the one of the guards uses a device that sends some kind of electric charge through his cuffs. We all watch as he falls to the floor, convulsing and moaning. The guards laugh and one says "That's your warning newbie, the next one will kill you." and they head out the doors, locking us in. As the door shuts, a hovering robot descends from the ceiling landing in the middle of us on the grass. A light on the top of the bot turns from red to green, instantly releasing the cuffs that bind us. Four more robots fall from the sky, all holding crates underneath them. The crates fall and expose weapons of all kinds inside.

The prisoners run to the crates at each corner. One hairy woman pushes me as the makes her way over to a crate, causing me to fall on my face. When I finally regain my composure I notice that everyone is already at a crate, picking their weapon of choice. I stand and run as fast as I can to the nearest crate and find that there are no weapons left.

I am not cut out for this.

I feel a tap on my shoulder and see Santos standing behind me, holding two older looking weapons similar to the ones I fought the Chronos with.

"Thanks" I say, taking the weapons from him.

I look around and notice that we're the only two people here from a tribe. Everyone else is a creature of some sort, like the ones I seen in that room on my way to the arena.

There are people that look like a mix of human and crow gathered in one corner. Their mysterious big black eyes taking in their surroundings. Skin almost the color of coal with wings protruding from their backs.

In another corner there's a group that reminds me of the characters in this book my brother use to read me. Werewolves I think they were called. Hairy people with crystal blue eyes who wear outfits made from barley wheat. Pointy teeth show as they talk amongst each other.

There is also an assortment of other characters. Some have horse bottoms and human tops. Others have gills in their necks, scales and large fish-like eyes. I stare in amazement at how many different people currently surround me that I never even knew existed.

A loud siren goes off and the environment instantly goes from day to night. Some of the creatures' eyes glow in the darkness, but other than that, its pitch black. Bright stars appear in the sky moments later illuminating the surrounding area. Deep in the distance I can see the top end of a moon that looks like it's being swallowed whole by the lake; casting a spotlight on the field.

"CLASS AGAINST CLASS" a loud automated voice says from the ceiling.

I look around and see that everyone is paired up with someone from their group. All holding weapons and facing each other in battle stance. I look over to where Santos was standing and see that he is also in fighting stance facing me.

"Let's go newbie!" he says, observing me in the moonlight.

"And what are we doing exactly?" I say, looking around to avoid his intimidating gaze.

"It's training time. The ones that pass the first round in The Dome have a chance to sharpen their skills before their next fight."

"The next fight! What if I don't want to fight again? I almost died the last time." I say, almost screaming.

"Calm down newbie. We fight less than the other competitors because they have to find at least two other tribe members for us to fight to make it fair. And as you can see, we're in short supply."

"I know that's supposed to make me feel better but it doesn't. And please stop calling me newbie, my name is Zaphora." I say, finally looking into his eyes.

I notice his look softens for a moment, but hardens again.

"Well come on Zaphora, let me see what you've got"

I take my stance and prepare for battle. What kind of luck do I have that I am the only one training with a man, let alone the champion of the tribe people for who knows how long. I shake my head at my circumstance and the automated voice comes on again.

"READY. BATTLE"

Santos takes a long stride towards me and swings one of his axes in my direction. I dodge the maneuver and stumble backward to regain my balance. I bring my right leg up to kick him in the stomach but he catches my foot and twists it, causing my whole body to twist and me to fall, landing on my knees.

I hop up and take my stance again. His leg lifts to kick me and I duck, swinging my leg around to him connecting with his face, but he never moves. Like a statue. He just glares at me with a hint of surprise in his eyes. I smile a little.

"Don't get use to hitting me newbie. You only connected because I allowed you to." He says in a stern voice, dropping his axes to the ground and changing his stance. Legs slightly apart. Hands behind his back. Chest out. Intense eyes.

I'm enraged. This time I use the hand-blade and aim for his chest. He grabs the blade with his hand and takes it from me. My foot flies towards his face, he grabs it, lifting me so high I lose my balance and fall on my back. I jump up and try again with the other hand-blade, this time aiming for his face. He grabs it and slices the bottom half of my shirt, just missing my skin. Never braking his gaze into my eyes. I back up and decide to regroup. Plotting my next move.

"There you go. You're too impulsive. Study your opponent. Find their strengths and use their weaknesses against them. I am able to combat your moves so well because I understand your fighting style. That of an untrained fighter."

"I'll have you know that I have been trained by the best warrior in our tribe. My brother Zeke taught me everything I need to know." I say with conviction.

"Well, that says a lot about your tribe." He says smirking a bit. "Have you ever been to battle? Have you ever killed someone for your tribe?"

"Well…. No." I say, looking down.

"Well there you have it." he says, laughing a little. "Wait. Did you say Zeke from the Seraphine tribe is your brother?"

"Yes, Why?"

He looks around to make sure no one's listening before walking closer to me. So close that I can feel his warm breath on my face. My heartbeat quickens. Not sure if it's out of fear or respect. Both things I rarely feel for someone.

"You're Lemak's daughter? The empress of the Seraphine tribe?" he whispers.

"Yes. How do you know my father?"

"Follow me." he says, grabbing my hand. We walk a couple of feet and disguise ourselves in the shadow of a large tree.

"How did you get here?" He says sternly.

"I was kidnapped during my spirit journey. How did you get here?"

"We don't have enough time for that story. Just know I've been here a long time. But I have met your brother."

"You've met my brother? Is he okay? Where is he? "

"He wondered into our village many years ago with eyes like portals that have seen much pain. After our elders deliberated, they decided that he could stay under our protection as long as he pulled his weight. Before I left he was a servant to one of the elders' families."

"Zeke," I say, holding back the tears welling in my eyes "is alive, and safe!"

That means the prophecy is coming to pass. And although I am thrilled my brother is alive, I'm equally as nervous of what else is to come.

Chapter 12

My small cot provides no relief after a long day in the training room. Every muscle in my body aches like it's never ached before. It's been weeks since Santos told me that my brother was alive. And he was been training me with intensity ever since. With Santos' help I began to learn how to survive in this nightmare.

I also learned the schedule we are to abide by in The Dunes.

Once a week all of the men and women are rounded up and taken to two large rooms where we are cleaned with powerful water hoses. We are then given semi-clean clothes and have 15 minutes to eat in our cells. We are only fed by the guards when our tournament day arrives. They make sure we are given a well-rounded meal so we don't pass out during battle and ruin their show. Other than that, we're on our own. Eating only what we are able to collect from the audience after every battle.
The prisoners from The Dunes battle once a week and the tribe members (Santos and I, and the poor souls they kidnap and force us to fight) only get to battle once a month. So far, not including my initial battle with Santee, I have been in two. In both battles, Santos came to my rescue and killed my opponent for me. The last time he whispered in my ear "Get it together Zaphora! You're not a newbie anymore. This is the last time I will save you. If you don't want to live, I won't make you." That was 3 weeks ago and my next tournament is 4 days away.

I close my eyes and all I can think of is Santos and how cruel his words were. I wonder how long he has been trapped here. Has this place made him this way or if he has always been this cold? Has tried to escape before? Is the scar on his face the result? Although he is one of the meanest people I've ever met, there is a softness to him. In his eyes, I can see his spirit is pure. Untarnished. Even through all of this. And I can't get him out of my mind. His skin, his eyes, his voice, make me feel like I have never felt before. My stomach growls and interrupts my thought process so I take out some more bread and cheese from the cooler and begin to eat.

Realizing for the first time that my food is in short supply, I take inventory of what I have left.

3 loafs of bread and 2 pieces of cheese.

Should be enough to get me through this week. I hope.

The sandman finds me shortly after, and for one, I'm grateful for the rest.

I'm lying in a field of white calla lilies. Thousands of them stretch in all directions. The beauty of it all is overwhelming. Standing to get a better view, I see that one a few feet away is not like the others. I walk closer and see a single black daffodil peeking through the calla lilies. I touch the petals and they all fall off. Sending a chain reaction to the lilies, causing them to turn into black daffodils and loose there petals as well. Before I can react I'm standing in a field of dead flowers. I try to run away from the eerie scene and can't move. The petals have turned into black quicksand and starts to swallow me whole. It moves so quickly that I have no time to stop it. It covers my eyes. Darkness.

"Rise and shine maggots! It's time for training!" a guard says outside my cell.

I open my eyes breathing heavily and sweating profusely. A black daffodil. I remember when I was learning about flowers and meanings from the Janti tribe that a black single daffodil symbolized misfortune. So what does a field of black daffodils symbolize? I shudder at the thought. I'm starting to get tired of these strange dreams.

"Ten minutes!" He says, running his hand across the bars of my cell. Lingering a little longer than I'd like.

I ignore his stare and begin with my daily routine. My first week here Santos started me on a strict schedule.

Wake up. Eat a handful of bread. Drink 5 handfuls of water. 50 jumping Jax. 50 push-ups. 50 sit-ups.

"Alright G.I. Jane, let's go!" the guard says outside my cell.

He must notice the confusion on my face, because he replies "Really tribee? You've never seen G.I. Jane? It's a classic!" he says, opening my cell.

I roll my eyes and stand against the wall. I hate this guard most of all. His protruding eyes roaming over my body like I'm a meal he wants to devour. The sour stench of hooch on his breath in the morning. And the odor that comes from his body, like he hasn't showered in months. I almost gag as he comes closer.

"Wow, you people really are sheltered. You can't even watch movies? How boring your lives must be." he says, placing the cuffs on my wrists. "Don't worry though. You play your cards right and maybe I'll take you to see one sometime." He smacks me on the butt before forcing me out of the cell. I bite my lip to the point of blood to prevent from head-butting him.

We pile in to the training room single file like every other day. But today the surroundings are different. Instead of the field we usually battle in, we are in a simulation of The Dome. There are even virtual people on the walls surrounding us.

"Listen up maggots! Today we're doing things a little different. Instead of your usual boring training exercises, we thought we would make you fight for your bunks tonight." A voice says over the loud speaker.

The other prisoners begin mumbles of fear and worry.

"What's going on?" I ask the Sophie. One of the prisoners I trained with a couple of times.

"They are making us fight to the death for a spot to sleep tonight." she says, placing a hand on my shoulder.

I can't lie, when we first met, her impressive fighting style created something in me I never thought I would experience, jealousy. I've never had to play second best to anyone, let alone another girl. But soon after I found her kindness a much needed comfort in a place filled with such dark energy.

"But why?" I say, looking around at the other frightened faces.

"Every so often they get an overwhelming number of complaints that there are too many people crowding the jail cells in the city. When that happens, they have us fight for our lives so that they can free up some space in our cells so that they can stick them down here with us."

"You've been through this before?" I say, still confused at what I'm hearing.

"Only once, and it wasn't nice. I was lucky and paired with a newbie, so I won my spot with ease, but others, like the girl who was in the cell next to mines, was paired with Shrika" she nods over in her direction "and she used to be a warrior before she was captured, so you know that didn't go well." she says, shaking her head at the memory.

I look at Shrika picking her teeth with one of her curved blades and hope I won't be so unlucky. But the way things are going, I doubt that'll be the case.

"You know the drill." says the man on the loud speaker. "Walk to the wall to your left and see who you are paired with. We will be here all night if needed people, so the sooner you get this over with the better."

"Good luck Z!" Sophie says with a slight smile and heads over to the wall.

I take my time walking to the list that will determine my future. Most of the prisoners nod at the list in approval of who they are paired with and stand off to the side readying their weapons. But there are a few who look scared, like lone gazelles in a room full of cheetahs. They try their best to hide it, but like animals, we can all smell their fear.

I'm determined not to be one of those people. Whatever this list says, I cannot show my fear. It'll be my demise.

When I finally get to the wall I see that I am paired with Helix. A Sintar with fierce eyes and menacing scowl that would frighten the bravest of men. In all the time I have been here, I haven't seen him say a word. Only stare. Like a wild animal waiting to be let out of its cage.

"You'll be fine Zaphora." Santos whispers in my ear "Just remember what I taught you about fighting styles. He's big and leaves his targets critically injured on impact. But he rushes his hits, so be sure to use that to your advantage. Don't allow him to touch you. Use your agility to your advantage." he touches my shoulder and is off to the corner to prep his weapon.

We are all given 5 minutes to sharpen our weapons, drink water, and prepare for the battle to come. I spend my time stretching and going over Santos' words. *'Use you're agility'*. And hope I'm fast enough to dodge his deadly blow.

When the alarm sounds, we take our place in the middle of the replicated Dome. Pairing off with our adversaries in a fight to sleep in our own cells tonight. The very thought would have been ridiculous to me just 3 months ago, but today, it's the only life I know.

A second alarm goes off after we are all in position and I watched in horror as one after another, lives are taken in the name of survival. Being in a ring with 3 other people doesn't come close to watching 50 people go head to head. Blood, wings, heads and even ears created a pool of sorrow beneath my feet.

But there's no time to mourn the lost. My arm begins to burn. My own little warning sign. And Helix is charging toward me. Before I know it he's in front of me. Aiming his massive spear directly at my neck. I dodge his attack. Barely. And make my own attempt to weaken him with a blow to the arm. Miss. This swing and miss routine goes on for some time. Sweat begins to build above his brow. He's slowing down. Getting tired.
I realize now why Santos had me stick to a strict routine every morning. To keep me agile. To enhance my strength.

He backs up. Dropping his spear to the side and removes a large blade from his back. Cheater! He swings in an upward motion on both of my sides. Trying to handicap me by cutting my arms off.

I've heard this is how he usually wins his fight. By catching his opponent off guard. They never see it coming. But I do.

I dodge his blows. Sidestepping around him. Slicing a nice chunk of back with one of my blades. The expression on his face is more than I could hope for. Surprise fills his eyes as he stumbles backward. If I die now, it would be worth it.

He catches me off guard and grabs my wrist. His grip so tight I drop one of my weapons.

This is it. I've failed. Spoke to soon. Now I will die.

He pulls me toward him. Spinning me so my back is to his chest. His breath is heavy and moist in my ear. My eyes close, awaiting the inevitable.

"I'm going to have fun with you little bunny." He whispers to me. My stomach is in knots. What does he mean?

I don't wait long to find out.

He secures my neck with his arm and begins to cut off my locks. I squirm and try to get away but he's too strong.

Fear and rage over come me. This can't be it. I won't let it be.

I hear Santos in my head *'Don't panic! Think about your next move.'*

I stop squirming and focus. Stab his leg with my other blade. He's distracted. Loosens his grip. I slide though. I'm free! But no time to celebrate. I turn and swing. Aiming for his throat. Right on target. Blood protrudes from his neck bathing me in red rain. I swallow my bile as I watch him gasp for air and grab his throat. He runs at me. Fury in his eyes. One hand extended toward my throat. I duck under his hand and stumble a few steps back. Just to be safe. But there's no need. He collapses. Staring at me as he falls. I watch as the life leaves his eyes.

Frozen. I stand there looking at his lifeless body before me. Not noticing everyone staring at me.

Judging me.

Zaphora.

The Killer.

Chapter 13

I come to and I'm sitting at the edge of the cot in my cell. My skin and clothes crusted over with Helix's blood. How long have I been sitting here?

There's another shirt and pair of pants sitting on top of the cooler. Good. At least I don't have to sleep in his blood.

I take the shirt off and stuff it under my bed, leaving only the sport's top I have on underneath. My pants don't come off as easy. They stick to my skin. Taking hair and skin with every tug. I finally remove them and toss them under my cot as well. My legs are on fire. Inside and out.

I will myself to the sink and begin to wash the blood off my skin. My blade slashing through his throat. The light leaving his eyes. It's all too much and tears fall at the thought.

You're a monster now. They've made you into a monster! How can you face you're father? You're mother? Yourself?

I stand there silently crying until all the tears are gone. When I regain my composure I take a deep breath and assess the damage.

The mirror above the sink reveals a paler version of the beautiful bronzed skin I use to love. My arms are scarred and bruised from months of fighting for my life. My hair is a mess. Although the locks in the middle are pretty much intact, most of the ones on the right side of my head have been chopped off. My eyes are cold. Empty. I'm empty.

Rite of Passage / New Earth Series Volume I

Unable to hold myself up any longer, I collapse. Give way to gravity. The floor is hard. I feel nothing. My body is in shock, numbing the pain of my flesh but not of my mind.

Who is this person I have become? This is not the woman I wanted to be. I have been so lost in the training. Lost in the survival of it all. I never stopped to realize that at one point training would end and reality would begin. I have taken a life. A creature of this earth is no longer breathing because of my hands. This is my reality now.

When sleep finally comes to me on the cold hard floor it's is of no relief. Different versions of me ending Helix's life slideshow through my closed lids. In one version I stab him though the heart. In another twisted version I pluck his eyes out of his skull. In all the dreams I'm smiling a sinister smile that scares me more than the multiple killings of Helix.

(BANG BANG BANG)

My eyes flutter open and I look around in panic. The numbness of my body is gone and the cold floor sends goosebumps through my damp skin. Smoke seeps through the bars of my cell and I can hardly breathe. Other prisoners are yelling and throwing things through their cages injuring some of the guards patrolling.

"Now!" a man's voice yells over the chaos.

The prisoners grab the guards near their cells and kill them in unison. Some with makeshift weapons. Others with bare hands. I pinch myself to make sure I'm awake. I am. The prisoners then begin to use the guard keys to unlock their cells and the ones around them. I jump up and put on the pants on the cooler at the end of my cot. I'm putting on the shirt when I notice Santos standing in front of my cell, unlocking the gate.

"After you…" He says, with a wave of his hand and sly smile.

"Thanks" I say back, as I leave the tiny box I thought I'd die in. "So how long have you been planning this?"

"For a couple of months now, ever since I found out who you….never mind." He says, looking away. "We're going to make our way to the training room before we leave and stock up on weaponry."

"Wait….What were…" I start.

"Come on, we have to hurry. We don't have much time." He says, taking my hand and pulling me toward the training room.

His big hands are calloused but still soft. Easily swallowing mines, and I feel like a child again. Timid and shy. Forgetting my train of thought, I follow him blindly into the smoke.

"I'm sorry this couldn't happen before the battle yesterday. We just couldn't risk trying to escape with 50 people and 20 guards. Half of the guards are still in the city picking up the new prisoners, so now was the perfect time to escape."

"I understand." I say but don't really mean. Killing Helix could have been avoided. My spirit could have remained pure. Fire brewed in the pit of my stomach but I worked hard to contain it.

We pass the training room and make a right. Heading toward a small black door in the hallway. Sophie walks to the front of the crowd, "Glad to see you're okay Z!" she says, giving me a slight shove as she passes me with the guard keys.

"Thanks, so am I." I say after her.

She makes it to the door and opens it to reveal a massive storage room of weapons and armor. We all file into the storage room and begin to equip ourselves.

"How did you know this is here?" I say to Santos. Astonished at how in sync everyone seems to be.

"I'll answer that." Tylo, the gossiping Sintar, says to Santos before turning to me "Long story short, Sophie has been having a relationship with one of the guards who was able to slip her the layout of The Dunes." He says winking at me.
Santos shoves him hard saying "Stay focused!"

They both look at each other for a long, uneasy second. I try to change the subject.

"So what is the plan after we get the weapons?" I ask, squeezing between them to pick up some daggers.

"There's a tunnel in the back of the training room that should lead to the outside." says Santos, getting back on topic.

"Wait! You mean to tell me we could have escaped weeks ago during training?"

"Well not weeks ago, maybe a couple of days ago. Shari has been working on that tunnel for months now, and everything had to be perfect for our escape. Including your skill level." He says, winking at me.

"Oh." I say, braking eye contact to hide my irritation.

After we equip ourselves with armor and weapons of choice, we make our way to the tunnel in the training room.

The tunnel is small and humid, causing the stench of the prisoners to linger longer than I would like. Only a small light held by the prisoner in the front guides our way. We duck walk for what seems like a mile before I see the moonlight cast a shadow on our bodies.

Once out of the hole I look around and see nothing but desert in every direction. Tears fall from my eyes as the fresh air dances in my lungs. Everyone begins running their separate ways, ecstatic at their newfound freedom. I look over at Santos for direction but he is counting the few stars left in the sky.

What I would give to know the world my father spoke of. A world where stars blanketed the skies at night, shining light on creature and human alike. How beautiful it must have been before the bombs destroyed the sky.

"This way." Santos affirms, pulling me out of my fantasy and back to reality.

Sophie runs to me and gives me an engulfing hug. "I'll miss you Z! Take care of yourself!" she says in my ear.

"Thanks Sophie, you too!" I respond. She runs south with a few other prisoners. Holding hands and laughing with the guard that helped us escape.

Rite of Passage / New Earth Series Volume I / 89

"Where are we going? I need to get back home. I need to tell my father Zeke is still alive!" I say as Santos grabs my hand and guides me north.

"You will, I promise. But first we're traveling north to the mountains to see my father."

I pull my hand away and stop to scowl at him.

"Calm down Zaphora, we'll get there, the mountains are on the way, trust me!"

My heart is torn in two. One part of me wants to go home and tell my father and mother that Zeke is alive and well while another part of me wants to make sure he is. The fact checker in me forces me to follow him. I have to be sure.

Chapter 14

We walk through the desert for what seems like an eternity before stopping to rest. Trying to cover as much ground as possible before sunrise. We come across a small abandoned shack and decide to hold up there during the hottest hours of the day before moving on.

"How did you know this was here?" I ask, stepping over some discarded wood.

"My brother, Tokala, and I used to come here from time to time to keep watch for our tribe. The solders of our village have the responsibility of maintaining the safety of everyone else. We would stay here to make sure that no one from The Dunes tried to sneak across and attack our people. As you can see, our truce with them was broken some time ago." Santos says, dusting off the old couch in the corner.

"Is that how you ended up there? In The Dunes?" I say, intrigued.

"Yes and no. After the truce was broken our lands were constantly being invaded by the people of The Dunes. In an act of desperation, my father sent me to see Shakira for guidance. She told me, in so many words, that the only way to stop the attacks on my village would be to fight in the Tournaments in The Dunes. She said that if I sacrificed myself, for as long as I needed to for the vision that I had to become a reality, that my village would be spared, and my family would not be harmed. So I did just that." he says, looking at me.

"Your vision? So you saw a vision when you went to see Shakira too?"

"Of course I did" he says laughing "That's kind of what she does. Shows you just enough of your spirit so that you know what to do when you can't figure it out yourself."

"What did you see? If you don't mind me asking."

"Well as you probably already know, it is hard to put into words. I did however encounter a strange feeling. A sort of peace that I never felt before at the end of the vision. It was the same feeling I felt when you told me who you were. And instinctively, I knew that it was time to leave. Like you were the reason I was there in the first place. I know that sounds crazy right?" he says, looking away from me.

"No, not at all." I say, blushing a bit. "I'm glad you were there. I don't know how I would have escaped without you."

"Don't mention it." He says, sitting in a broken chair next to the window. "Look, you should probably get some rest. We still have a long way to go and you need all of your strength. Sleep on the couch and I'll keep watch. I'll wake you when it's time to go."

"Sounds good. Thanks. But I think I'm going to freshen up first. Do you know if there's any water around here?"

"Under the floorboards of the sink in the bathroom. There should be a couple of jugs left. Help yourself."

"Thank you." I say, and make my way to the bathroom.

Lifting the floorboard, I take out a jug of water and wash up. I then drench my hair and pick up one of the daggers I took from the weapon room. My shaky hand attempts to cut the wayward locks on my scalp. After 3 unsuccessful tries I walk out of the bathroom and look over at Santos.

"Hey Santos, would you mind? I can't go any further with my hair looking like this."

He grins a little and motions for me to come over. I sit on the floor in front of him while he shaves the cut locks off of my head. As I watch them fall my heart commences in breaking into a thousand little pieces. I've grown these locks for years. Nurtured and cared for them, only to have them cut off in an instant. I take deep breaths with every cut to prevent myself from freaking out. He finishes, leaving only a patch of locks going down the center of my head. He hands me the knife and says "I hope I didn't mess it up too bad."

"No worse than Helix did." I say, standing.

"I kind of like it. It gives you an edgy look." He says grinning at me.

I cut my eyes at him and return back to the bathroom to assess the damage. This person in the mirror is so far from what she use to be. I allow a couple of tears to fall for her. The innocent girl on the spirit journey. Then secure the locks at the top of my head and wipe my face.

I am no longer the person I knew. How can I be? Now that I know what's out here. The creatures and evil that live in this world. There is no room for the girl that grew up in The Greenlands in this world that I know now. She was a lie. The only truth is the woman staring back at me now.

Chapter 15

It takes no time for me to drift off to sleep on the old dusty couch. I was so exhausted from our midnight escape that before I knew it, Santos was waking me up.

"Zaphora. Get your things, it's time to go."

I nod back at him, groggy eyed, and lift my heavy body off the couch. My weapons seem to weigh 80 pounds on my already exhausted frame.

Santos picks up a cotton scarf and coat made of fox fur and tosses it to me. "Put this on, it's going to be chilly."

I put on the coat and scarf and notice Santos has on a coat as well.

"Where did these come from?" I say, putting the hood on my head.

"I stored a couple of supplies before I went to The Dunes." he says, picking up a sac and his weapons.

"Even though you didn't know if you were ever going to get out of there?"

"Yeah, well my father taught be always to have a plan B. Plan A's tend to get a little complicated sometimes."

"Tell me about it." I say, following him out the door.

The desert wind hits us with a vengeance, blowing the hood off my head as soon as I close the door. I secure the scarf over my nose and mouth and pull the hood over my head before following behind Santos on the long journey ahead.

We walk for miles before Santos agrees to stop and take a break. He tosses me a bottle of water and I relish in the comfort of quenching my thirst momentarily.

"The sun is setting. Where will we make camp for the night?" I say, looking around.

"We're not making camp for the night. That's why I let you sleep so long. In order for us to reach the next suitable place to rest, we need to walk through the night."

"Walk through the night! We can barely see at night. How will we know where to go?"

"I know this sky like the back of my hand. You couldn't ask for a better navigator." he says, winking at me.

"Yeah, well, what about the creatures in the sand? I've been told that the sand creatures are the most dangerous at night."

"That doesn't concern me." He says, waving me off "And it shouldn't concern you either by the way you handled Helix." he says laughing. "What does concern me, however, is if we burn alive in the sun because we have no shelter. Now let's go, we still have a lot of ground to cover."

The memory of what I did to Helix hits me like a ton of bricks. His cold, dead eyes looking up at me. I shake off the ill feeling the best I can and follow behind Santos.

Hours pass and day turns to night as we walk deeper into the unknown. The sandstorm has stopped but the chill of the night air keeps the scarf over my mouth and hood covering my head. Memories of my family, friends and village keep me company. But it's not long before visions of The Dome and Helix enter my mind, causing me to stumble and fall. Santos never turns around. He is focused on the night sky and the direction we are headed. I pick myself up and start walking again.

The skin on my left shoulder blade starts to sting and makes my eyes go blurry with tears. I told Santos this was a bad idea! Now, after escaping the Dome from hell I'm going to be eaten by a sand creature.

A cold gust of wind hits the back of my neck and causes me to shiver. I look behind me, embracing myself for the inevitable and see a big cloud of smoke heading for us.

Oh no. This is much worse. Not again. Not Now.

"Santos!" I scream as loud as I can. He finally diverts his eyes from the sky ahead and they widen at the black fog behind me.

"Black magic! Zaphora, we've got to move. Fast." he says, running to me.

He grabs my hand and we take off.

The fog covers us whole. Making it impossible for us to see where we're headed. We stop running. Not wanting to go too far in the wrong direction.

"Zaphora, your eyes..." Santos says, staring at me.

A gust of wind pushes me back and I fall, releasing Santos' hand. I jump up, readjusting my bad and weapons and he is nowhere to be found.

"Santos!!!!!" I scream in panic.

The burning on my shoulder magnifies, paralyzing my left arm with pain. I lift my hand to feel where the pain is coming from and scratch my arm. My nails protrude like claws from my hands. Blood drips down my arm and falls to the sand. The fog concentrates on the blood in the sand. Lifting the sand it landed on before evaporating into the sky.

A few feet away Santos passed out in the sand. My feet move me before I can think and before I know it I'm at his side. I rock him back and forth trying to wake him, but he never opens his eyes. "Santos. Santos, wake up!"

I open the bottle of water and pour it over his face and he jerks into consciousness.

"What......what was that!" he says, still trying to regain composure.

"I wish I could tell you." I say, standing up next to him "All Shakira was able to tell me is that it's some sort of relative of mines that has it out for me."

"Well, I could gather that by the aggressive attack. We were taught much about black magic when I was growing up, but that isn't what I'm referring to. You........you were different. Your eyes were lighter, you had claws, and your back was glowing. What was that?"

Rite of Passage / New Earth Series Volume I

"I don't know. This is the second time that has happened to me. I think it only happens when danger is near."

"That can't be it, otherwise it would have happened every time you were in The Dome, and this is my first time seeing it. That was something else. Something I've never seen before."

"I......I don't know." I say, shaking my head.

"Do you know who is attacking you?" he says, beginning to walk again.

"No, Shakira wasn't able to tell me that." I say, walking next to him "She just knew it was someone related to me. But I can't think of anyone that I know who would want to bring me harm. My tribe are a peaceful people. After the war we only practice peace and forgiveness with our fellow tribe members."

"Is that what they told you?" Santos says, laughing. "Man I can't wait for you to meet my father. It's like you've been under a rock for 18 years. You're thoughts are still so naïve, even after all you've witnessed. And your tribe. Ha. Your tribe that is far from peaceful."

"What are you talking about? I will agree that the people of The Dunes were what you would call savages, but my people are far from that! We are one with the earth and take pride in being so close to the Mother. And how would you know anything about my people anyway? Your tribe was exiled nearly 20 years ago. So you can't possible know what goes on where I'm from."

"I know more that you can imagine. Especially since our fathers were best friends before our tribe was exiled to live in the mountains. He'll tell you all about your peaceful tribe and its leaders in due time."

"Why can't you just tell me now what you think you know about my tribe?" I shout, angrily.

"Because it is not my place to share the stories of the old world. That is a job held by the elders."

"The elders?"

"Yes, the elders. They are wise men, appointed by the heavens to remember, record, and share our peoples past. My father was one of the first appointed so you will get to hear the history of what happened to our people, and of your people, from one of the wisest elders."

Elders? Why have I never heard of such a people? We were taught our history by our parents not individuals appointed by the "heavens". Whatever that is. Wait. I think I recall heaven being mentioned in our history lessons. Something about where you go after you die I think. But what does that have to do with the appointing of Elders? I wonder how much of what they believe is different from what I've been taught. Whose belief is the truth? There's already a whole other land with creatures that I was never even told about in my tribe. How much more have they kept from me? Do they even know about those people? And if they do know, why would they purposely send me on this quest if they knew that it was dangerous? The farther I travel, the more confused I feel.

Chapter 16

Night becomes day as we walk the endless sands in silence. I try my best to prepare myself for the meeting with Santos' father tomorrow but nothing I do calms my nerves. Everything I've ever known, everything I've been taught feels like a lie. Santos must see the uneasiness in my face because he turns and places a hand on my shoulder.

"I know you must be losing your mind right now, but trust me, everything will make sense tomorrow. Just try to focus on the beauty that is around you. The earth beneath your feet. The air entering your lungs. It'll help." he says with a smile.

I smile at his words of encouragement and try to let the thoughts of worry get lost in the sand.

Up ahead the sand gives way to a small cave surrounded by several cactuses. We make it inside just as the heat is becoming unbearable. I sit on a rock near the center of the cave and Santos sits next to me. Handing me some bread and water he pulls out of his bag. The sight of food instantly makes my stomach growl and I devour the bread faster than I mean to.

"Try to get some rest. We'll leave in a couple of hours and make our way to the mountains." He says, laying on his bag.

"I can't really sleep. Anticipation I guess. But you can go ahead and get some rest, I'll keep watch."

"If you insist. Wake me before the sun sets." he says, turning his back to me.

Rite of Passage / New Earth Series Volume I / 100

I make my way to the edge of the cave and sit in the doorway. A snake crawls a few feet from me in the sun, temporarily preoccupying my thoughts.

I look over at Santos and see his body almost stretches from one wall of the cave to the other. I never really noticed how big he was until this very moment. His breath is heavy and short when he sleeps, like he is always fighting, even in his dreams.

I trace the tattoos that mark his arms with my eyes and think of how different his life must have been from mines. Some of the scars that mark his skin look older and engraved like birthmarks. He tells stories of his village at war; of spending months at a time with his brother in the desert as a solder. Away from his family, away from his home. Of sacrificing himself for his village; and I suddenly feel selfish for focusing on my own problems.

The snake outside the cave is closer now and seems to be heading right for me. It stops a few feet away and lifts its head looking into my eyes.

"Zzzzzaphora" it hisses at me. "Don't trust what you hear. Only what you know."

"What I know? I suddenly feel like I know nothing of this world." I say, louder than I mean to, causing Santos to shift a bit behind me. I lower my voice and continue "I am sick and tired of everyone telling me what I should believe! I should be allowed to make my own judgments of what I choose to believe after I'm given the whole truth. Not peoples versions of it!"

"I know your pissssssssed, but remember, everyone has a motive. And your involvement in their fight is of upmost importancccccce to them. Just remember, you already know, inssssssside, all you need to know to make your decision. Just trust yoursssself." the snake hisses and slivers away, disappearing behind a cactus.

Fight? What fight? The war is over. It ended 25 years ago. And Santos ended the war between his people and the people of the Dunes when he sacrificed himself. Maybe his involvement with breaking me out of that prison is going to start another war. That last thing I want is to be the cause of more damage to the Mother.

My mind works in overdrive trying to untangle the snakes' message and before I know it the sun is setting. I stretch and gather my belongings before waking Santos. He takes no time to adjust back to reality. Quickly grabbing his bag and weapons before heading out of the cave.

As we walk toward the mountains, I notice the terrain around us begins to change. The sand begins to give away to concrete and rock. To the left a couple of miles down I can see what looks like a stream flowing parallel to us. A dormant volcano appears behind some clouds in the horizon. Filling the once clean air, and my lungs, with ash and smoke. The flat surface I started to become accustom to walking on begins to transform into hills and valleys of stone in every direction. The combination of these changes in atmosphere make it harder for me to breathe.

"We're not far now" Santos says, looking back at me "Watch your step, the deeper we get into the mountains, the steeper they will become."

I nod and try and focus again on my breathing. The thick air fights with every inhalation to fill my lungs. Santos turns and notices my struggle and we stop to take a break.

"Sorry, I forgot you're not use to this climate. Being from The Greenlands, I bet it is easier to breathe growing up around all those trees and flat land." he says chuckling "This, on the other hand is where warriors are born. Where survivors are made. If you can make it here, you can make it anywhere."

His words are unsettling. Warriors and survivors. Grim skies and ash rocks. None of this is what I expected it to be. Although I'll admit, I didn't know what to expect exactly. And after that conversation I had with the snake a couple of hours ago, I could be walking into an ambush for all I know.

I try to calm my thoughts and remember that anything has to be better than that hell I was just locked in. Those tiny cells made of concrete and stone mocking my very existence. Causing a peace of me to die with every battle I was forced to fight. Nothing, not even this, can be worse than that.

The closer we get to where Santos calls home, the gloomier the skies become. The burnt aroma of ash assaults my nose with no mercy. If what was described to me as hell was true, this would truly be hell on earth. The lake that was in the distance before now flows next to us as we travel. At first sight it looks like a normal lake, but at further investigation, you can see a red bubbling substance just below the surface.

"What is that?" I say to Santos through the scarf over my mouth.

He follows my eyes to the lake and says "Oh, that's Orafiss, or "Dragon's Blood" is what the kids like to call it."

"Dragon's Blood? There are dragons here? Like in the myths I've been told about?" I ask, mystified.

"Well, that's the legend anyway. When we first settled here we drank the water not knowing that the Orafiss was traveling through the lake. Some of our tribe members died from the effects. Others adapted to the change it created in our bodies in different ways. Some were effected in their skull, causing the bones to deform and create horns that protrude from their foreheads. Others shoulder blades were effected, causing them to develop strange wings. And others, known as Blazers, are able to control the fire element. Giving weight to the theory that the Orafiss is truly dragon's blood, but I think it's just some sort of mutated lava. I mean we do stay near a dormant volcano. But the people will believe whatever tale makes them sound cooler."

"Wait what?" I say, stopping in my tracks. "That's a lot of information you just threw at me all nonchalantly like it's no big deal. So you're telling me that everyone in your village is deformed in some way?"

"Well when you put it like that I guess it does sound bad. But we don't choose to look at it in that way. What others see as misfortune we see as strength, and we find ways to use those strengths to our advantage. The horns, for example, can be used in battle when there are no weapons present to end a life. The wings, can be used to scout a coming invasion, and travel at faster speeds. And I don't have to tell you how awesome it is to have the ability to control fire." he says, winking at me.

"I....I guess you're right. I didn't mean to offend you or your people. It's just a lot for me to take in, that's all." I say, smiling a little to ease the tension.

"It's fine. I know you're overwhelmed. I'll try to take it easy on you. At least until we reach the village." he says, giving me a playful shove.

Chapter 17

We reach the village shortly after nightfall. The Orafiss makes the water glow a pretty orange in the moonlight. Drawing closer I hear children laughing and playing, and people singing what sounds like an old hymn. I strain to make out the words and realize that I know the song that they're singing. My mother use to sing it to me as I fell asleep.

Zhee shaaaa van deeeeee, la miiiii pha siiiiiii, Looooo kneeeee sjooooo, loooooo kneeeee sjoooooo. (We give thanks for life. We give thanks for love. We honor you. We honor you).

The song brings a tear to my eye. I swallow hard, trying to rid myself of the lump welling in my throat.

The smell of pork and potatoes overwhelm my senses, making my mouth water at the thought of a meal other than bread and cheese.

We reach a gate made of wood and twine with two guards patrolling the front. As we walk closer, I hear one of the guards yell "What business do you have at this village?"

"I came to make your wife an honest woman!" Santos yells back, laughing.

"Santos!" the guard yells and runs over to us. They embrace so hard all I can think of is how bruised their chests will be in the morning. Then they commence to doing some sort of tribal hand greeting before Santos turns to me and says "This is Zaphora, daughter of Lemak. Zaphora, this is my brother Tokala."

I extend my hand "It's a pleasure to meet you."

"Zaphora" he says, taking my hand and kissing it "Daughter of Lemak. What are you doing Santos, collecting all the children of the Seraphine tribe?" He says, looking back at Santos.

"Don't pay this jokester any mind, as you can see, the water has seeped into his skull." Santos says, tugging at Tokala's horns.

"Yeah, I'm sure hot hands over here told you he got the better deal, with the whole being able to control fire thing," he says, bating Santos' hand away "but I am still the better warrior little brother, and these horns only further prove that point." He says, tugging at his own horns. "Come. Father will be happy to hear of your safe return." He says walking toward the fence.

Santos can control fire? I wonder why he never used it in the arena for protection. This is already shaping out to be an interesting night.

We walk into the gates and everyone in sight rushes to Santos. Some picking him up off the ground, others patting him on the back. Some even cry at the sight of his homecoming. I look around and notice how close everyone is and it makes me miss my home. My family.

The cobblestone is a welcome change to the dirt and rocks wreaking havoc on my feet on the way here. The village resembles that of a small city. Different sized buildings decorate the streets and are lit by large lanterns. In the center of the village is a thin, elderly woman with horns passing out plates of food to the people passing by. A large well is a couple of feet away where the people who have just grabbed their plate, wait in line to grab a cup of water. Children run wild in every direction, occasionally being told by an elder to 'slow down' or 'be careful'.

I think of Zeke and begin to look for his face in the swarm of strangers. I expect to be frightened of the people in this village, but instead I am sympathetic to them. With all the things they have been through, both mentally and physically, they are still strong. Still loving. Still accepting. They are nothing like the stories I have been told about them.

A little girl with small wings on her back runs up to me. "Hi! I'm Sharine, what's your name?" she says eagerly.

"Hello Sharine, it's nice to meet you." I say kneeling down to her level "My name is Zaphora."

"Hi Zaphora! Your hair is funny looking. Did you cut it that way?" she says touching the locks hanging over my shoulder.

"Well, yes..." I say, stopping to form the right words "I.."

"Sharine! Leave that nice woman alone." an older woman says, making her way over to us in long strides. Her shawl floating behind her.

Her cat-like eyes are calculating. Sizing me up the closer she gets to me. Her face is strong but beautiful. She reaches for Sharine and pulls her to her side. A small dragon tattoo peeks a little through her shawl.

"Hello, I am Kamenna, one of the leaders of this tribe. And you are?" She says, raising her eyebrow at me.

"Zaphora" I say, extending a hand to her "My people are from the Seraphine Tribe."

She shakes my hand "Zaphora? Daughter of Lemak?" She studies my eyes.

"Yes." I say, pulling my hand back.

"Well, you're far from home aren't you?" she says with a smirk. "Come my dear, let's head to the Great Room and get you warm."

She turns and I follow behind her sure stride and stiff long braid to one of the structures a few feet away. Mid-stride, Kameena lets go of Sharine's hand and she runs off to play with the other children. Turning to wave at me before she goes. Her shiny black curls bouncing as she chases another little boy with horns around the well.

We pass a large bonfire with at least 20 people surrounding it sharing tales of war and battle before we reach the large stone structure with double doors made of large rocks and dirt.

Great Room indeed. I'm taken back by how large and beautiful the room is when the guards open the doors for us. Decorated with art and beautiful rugs, this room reminds me of my brief studies of old world museums. Two large wooden chairs center the room, each covered in bear fur. To my left is a small table with two chairs made of mahogany. To my right is another room a few feet away with a large table in the center, and three men, two with horns, one with wings, surrounding it and talking. Kamenna shoots them a look as we enter and the man with the wings quickly closes the door.

A small woman with big black eyes and skin the color of coal enters the room holding a tray of food and two rose colored drinks. She stops a few feet short from Kamenna and bows.

"Greetings Kamenna and guest" she says looking me up and down. "Would you like some food or drinks to nourish your appetite this evening?" she says, extending the tray.

"I'm alright for now Zita, thank you. You may help yourself Zaphora." Kamenna says, walking toward a table and chairs to our left.

"Thank you." I say, grabbing a plate and a drink.

"Come Zaphora, have a seat." Kamenna says as she sits at the table.

I walk over and sit across from her, placing my bags at my feet. There is a long silence while I eat my food. Even though I am consumed with the hole I'm filling in my stomach, I can feel heat of Kamenna's eyes on me. Studying my every move. I take a break from my food and take a sip of the rosy drink, catching her eyes with mines. She smiles slightly, enhancing her prominent cheekbones, and finally speaks. "So what's a beautiful girl like you doing so far away from home?"

I swallow the rest of the fruity drink in my mouth before I answer "I was on my spirit journey when I was kidnapped by a man with two mouths and sold to fight in The Dunes."

Saying it out loud sounds crazier than it was actually living through it. Like one of those unbelievable folk tales I've been told. The woman and the beast with two mouths. The thought makes me laugh a little to myself.

"Is that where you met my son, Santos?" she says, never taking her eyes off of mines.

"Yes. He saved me. If it weren't for him I would either be dead or still trapped there. I owe him my life."

"I see..." She says, clasping her hands together on the table.

I start to eat the rest of my food in silence as she watches every movement. Her glare is so penetrating that I can swear she's causing sweat beads to appear on my forehead. "So….. Santos told me that my brother Zeke was here. Is that true?" I say, breaking the uncomfortable silence.

"He is indeed. Around this time he's usually training in our arena. If you are done with your meal, I can take you to him." she says standing.

"I am. Thank you!" I say, hopping out of my chair and swooping my bags up in one quick motion.

"Very well then. Follow me." she says, floating towards a small wooden door tucked in the back of the room.

Her resemblance to Santos is uncanny. They both carry themselves like warrior Gods. Strong and cunning. Always ready for battle. They also share the same deep set copper eyes. Cautious and calculating. Always analyzing, friend or foe, never quite fully trusting anyone.

Her steps are light and soundless, like a cat in the night. Taking in every sound around her and storing it in some important/non-important memory bank in her mind. Or at least that's what I imagine she's doing by the way she moves.

She's about 3 inches taller than I am so her long strides make it hard for me to keep her pace. We walk through the door and down a sand paved path until we reach an enclosed area made of trees. The entrance has two lit torches on either side.

"Zeke, my dear, there is someone here to see you." Kamenna says as she passes through the torches.

I squint in the barely lit arena looking for who she's speaking to. There are at least 20 men, and some boys, training and fighting one another. One walks toward us.

"Zeke?" I say, barely above a whisper.

He jogs closer and I see his hazel eyes. My father's flat nose and mother's thin lips. It's Zeke!

"Zaphora?" He says, darting toward me, lifting me off the ground with his embrace.

And I can't take it. I can't breathe. I finally fall apart and weep in my brothers arms.

Chapter 18

We hold each other and I cry until my body is drained of all its tears. By this time Kamenna is long gone and the people training have gone back to what they were doing before our big emotional scene.

"Look at you! You're a woman now!" He says pulling back "I never thought I would see you again!"

"I know, me either!" I say, drying my eyes with my shirt. "Wow, you're huge!" I say, touching his buff arm, "When did you become such a warrior?"

He laughs "When did I become a warrior? I've always been a warrior! Taught you everything you know." He says, giving me a light shove.

"Yeah, well….You know what I mean. You weren't in this kind of shape before. I wouldn't have recognized you had it not been for those big ears and our father's nose." I say, laughing at the jokes I used to tell about those ears.

"Very funny."

"But seriously," I say, changing my tone "What happened to you that day? Why did you just leave us? Why did you leave me?"

He sighs "Zaphora, it's more complicated than that. What happened to me…..I wasn't sure who I could trust. Especially our father. He is not who you think he is."

Deja Vu

"What do you mean?" I ask confused.

He wraps his arm around my shoulder and leads me to a bench near the edge of the training area "You might want to have a seat. This is going to be a lot to take in."

We sit on the bench and he begins "On the day I disappeared, I was up before the sunrise preparing to hunt for our village like any other day. On this particular day, I went to wake you but father stopped me and said that I should let you sleep because you stayed up late the night before studying. I was hesitant to let you slide, knowing you needed more practice but father insisted so I went without you. "

I shake my head, feeling the tears welling in my eyes. The anger I had and still have for myself for not being there for him is ever present in this moment.

He continues "I'd just finished setting up the traps when I heard a noise behind me. I turned, bow in hand. Ready to kill whatever game came my way. Instead I stood face to face with a man that seemed to glow in the darkness. His eyes held me in some sort if trance as he lowered my bow. His ears were large and pointy. And although he had a few wrinkles on his face, he looked nothing like any elder that I had ever seen before."

"Did he look like" I lower my voice to a whisper "like he could be from here?"

"No. Not from here. All I can remember before he knocked me out with some sort of dust was the look in his beady black eyes. Those eyes still hunt my dreams to this day." he says, shaking his head at the thought "When I awoke, I was in a bright white room. Laying on a table next to a big complicated looking machine. When I tried to get up to run, a small shock was sent to my spinal cord, pulling me back onto the table. The room was so bright that I could only see the machine next to me and the white cloth covering the lower half of my body. I tried to scream, to call for help, but nothing responded. Not even an echo."

He looks down at his feet and fidgets with his hands "I stayed there. Locked in that white room for who knows how long. I had no since of time. No human interaction. No hope. Only that big white room and my thoughts."

"That sounds like torture!" I say.

"I thought so too until I experienced what came next. One day, out of the blue, the machine next to me begin to beep loudly. When it stopped, the table started slowly draining what looked like blood and some white misty substance from my spinal cord." He looks up at me before continuing, "It was the most painful thing I've ever felt. I knew I was dying. Slowly and painfully. My skin began to wrinkle, and my muscles ached. The pain was so excruciating at times that I would just black out."

"I'm so sorry Zeke." I say, tears streaming down my cheeks.

He places one of his hands on my back and rubs reassuringly, then continues "After one of my blackouts, I awoke to a tall beautiful woman with the same features as the man who took me, standing over me. Her voice was so soothing that I thought for sure she was a hallucination. But when she lifted my fragile body off the table, without the shock going to my spinal cord, I knew she must be real. She practically carried me out of the big white room while I struggled to clear my blurry sight and regain the feeling back into my legs. She gave me a vile of some green liquid and told me to drink it. I did, and my body begin to heal itself instantly. Once my vision was clear, I could see dozens of big white rooms in every direction. All with other young men lying tables like the one I had been on. I asked the lady why we weren't saving the others and she said that there was only time to save me. That I, Zeke, the brother of Zaphora, is the only one that matters."

"Wait. What? How did she know your name? Or who I am for that matter?" I ask, shaking a little.

"I asked her that same thing. She said that there was no time to tell me but that we would all meet again. Then she told me that I'm to travel north, to the Alki Mountains, until you arrived. So that's what I did. And I've been here ever since."

"I don't understand. Why didn't you come back home? Father taught us how to always find our way home by following the sunset. Why didn't you come back to us? They held a funeral for you and everything." I say, almost screaming.

"Calm down Zaphora. It wasn't my choice." he says, placing a hand on my shoulder, "That was my first thought too. But as I was leaving the woman told me something that made me come straight here. She said that our father was the reason I was taken. That he had me go into the woods that morning on my own, well aware that I would be taken and brought to that horrible place."

"Why would you believe her? You just met this woman and because she helped you escape you decide to follow her instructions blindly and abandon your family?"

"No, I believed her because of what she showed me."

"Showed you? What could she possible have shown to you to make you not want to come back home?"

"It was a flood of images. Our father speaking and shaking hands with the tall man with the pointy ears. Our father up before sunrise staring at me while I slept the morning I left. Now when have you ever known father to be up before the sun?"

"No time that I can remember. Mother usually has to put a cold towel on his face to wake him up. And that's usually after the sun is in the middle of the sky."

"Exactly! Which made me start to think about some other things that didn't add up. In every training we have ever had to go to, when have you ever heard him say it's okay not to go because you didn't receive enough sleep the night before. Think about it Zaphora. We are responsible for the livelihood of our tribe. Slacking off or not showing up has never been an option for us. And on top of all of those red flags he gave me a hug before I left."

"He hugged you? He's never hugged you! He used to say that a man hugging a boy only weakens him." I say confused.

"Right! So you see Zaphora, I had no choice but to follow her instructions at least until I found out more about what happened that day. I couldn't risk going back and falling into the same trap I did before."

"I have so many questions, and not enough answers." I say "Why you? Why would he do that to you? To our family?" I say, shaking my head "And why did she save you? Not that I'm not grateful. But why you out of all the other people being held captive there?"

"I don't know Z. But I think I know someone who might. Let's go see Kanen."

Chapter 19

We rise off of the bench and begin to walk.

"Who is Kanen?" I ask.

"He's the leader of this tribe. His wife, Kamenna, brought you to the arena to see me." Zeke says, smiling at me.

"So he's Santos' father?"

"Yes, Santos and Tokala are his sons. He was the one that convinced the people of this village to allow me to stay. He has treated me with nothing but respect since the day that I came to his gates."

"Did he tell you that he was best friends with our father before their tribe was exiled?" I say in a hushed tone.

"Sure he did. I believe that's part of the reason he allowed me to stay. Out of love and respect for our father. He is a good man Z. Nothing like the menacing stories we've heard about him back at home."

"I don't know Zeke. They sure do spend a lot of time talking about wars and training for battle. Are you sure they can be trusted? They just seem so different from our tribe." I say, looking around to make sure no one heard me.

"Of course I do. Kanen has been very transparent with me. He and his people have accepted me, and will accept you, with open arms."

"So why haven't you asked him why our father did this to you?"

"I did, shortly after I arrived. He said that I wasn't strong enough to bear that burden yet, and that I should come back when the time was right. And I can't think of a better time than now, can you?" he says, smiling in my direction.

"Nope, I guess not." I say shrugging.

"What's happened to you? You're a lot more guarded than I remember."

"It's a long story." I say with a sigh "I'll tell you about it tomorrow. But for now, let's focus on getting some answers from Kanen."

We make our way back down the sandy path to the Great Room. Zeke opens the back door for me as we enter and I stop to watch Santos, Tokala and their parents talk joyfully in the middle of the room. The resemblance is obvious now that they're all standing side by side. Santos and Tokala could be twins if Tokala was two shades lighter and a little taller. I almost have a hard time spotting Santos, who seems to have taken a bath and trimmed his long beard into a tapered goatee. His cleaner look reveals how attractive he is under all that hair. My heart flutters a bit at his eyes connecting with mines across the room.

Zeke walks ahead of me and stops a few feet away and salutes. Awaiting a nod from Kanen before walking over to the group.

So he's a member of their army now? I guess I'm not the only one who's changed. Zeke used to teach me that it was wrong to take a life. Especially for someone else's fight. But I guess a lot changes when you need to survive.

"Good evening all." He says, looking around to everyone in the group "I was wondering if my sister Zaphora and I can have a word with you this evening sir?" He focuses now directly on Kanen who looks over at me still standing by the door.

"So you're Zaphora? Come closer my dear, I'm not going to bite." Kanen says.

"Contrary to popular belief." Tokala chimes in, and they all laugh.

I make my way over to Kanen, and extend my hand to shake his. He takes my hand and kisses it, catching me off guard. "You look very much like your mother." He says, looking into my eyes.

"Thank you." I say, thinking that that complement has always been given to my brother instead of me. Outside of her demeanor, I don't think that my mother and I really have anything; including our features in common.

"If you'll excuse us my dear." Kanen says to Kamenna.

"Sure my beloved. I will take the boys to get something to eat. We have a lot of catching up to do." she says, looping her arms with Santos and Tokala's as they walk away, disappearing through a large wooden door in the back of the room.

Kanen turns and walks towards a room with a lion's head mounted over the door. He takes a small key from around his neck and unlocks the door. The bright white light on the other side nearly blinds me as we enter. When my eyes readjust, I notice we are now standing in an all-white room, that is shaped like an egg. We are on some sort of platform that winds as far up as my eyes can see. The center of the room holds a large glass bubble that immediately brings back bad memories of The Dunes. I wipe my sweaty palms on my pants and force that nagging feeling back down to the pit of my stomach. The bubble has men, women and other creatures inside working on large machines that barely glance up at us as we walk by.

I look over at Zeke who's now stern faced and walking stiffly between me and Kanen. He feels me looking and returns my uneasy stare. Then gives me a reassuring two tugs on his shirt, a signal we use to have when he was teaching me how to hunt. A reminder that he would never let anything happen to me.

We turn down a small corridor and stop in front of a metal door with a glass nob. Kanen places his finger on the knob and a drop of his blood falls into the knob; turning it from clear to red before opening. Inside the room is a large glass table and four hovering silver chairs. The door closes softly behind us and the stark white light becomes a soft glowing green; causing my heartbeat to decrease immediately into a calmed state. Zeke's muscles are also relaxed now but his eyes have the same since of alertness which eases my mind a little.

Kanen sits on one of the chairs and beacons for us to join him. Zeke and I look at each other and back at Kanen skeptically. Kanen responds "Don't worry, their just chairs. Sit so we can have our discussion. I promise, they're the most comfortable chairs you'll ever sit on." He then gestures again to the chairs with a warm smile. Zeke sits first and then gives me a nod that it's safe.

Once we are all seated, I ask "What is this place? Who are those people outside?"

"We're in my headquarters. This is where I hold all of my important meetings and research about our past, present and future."

"But this technology," I say, looking around, "It's supposed to be outlawed. Why are you killing our Mother with this wastefulness?"

"You have it all wrong Zaphora. I am not killing our Mother, the contrary is true. I'm revitalizing her."

"What do you mean?"

"You see, after the war.......Maybe this would be better received if you heard it from some people you trust."

'Heard what?"

"The truth." He says then taps the table 3 times and the lights dim to a softer glow. Three holograms appear in the middle of the glass table and I almost fall off of the hovering seat.

It's can't be...... Graced Zyere! Jacobie! Jaielle! And Grandfather???

"What kind of evil is this? You're all dead! How are you doing this?"

"It is not evil Zaphora. It's Science. You're father and I were hunting in the woods one day and discovered some technology that we thought for sure was extinct. This is that technology. It's what we use to call a program back in the old world. But this program was like no other; it has the ability to allow us to communicate with spirits that have already passed onto another realm."

"But why would you need such technology? The Janti tribe members are capable of doing that without the help of some machine that is damaging our Mother!"

"The Janti tribe, unlike this technology, has one fatal flaw. It's human. And since the beginning of time there have been men who live to exploit people and their connections with those in the other realm for their own benefit. This program on the other hand is not just a messenger, it is the spirit itself interacting with the system in a way that we in this realm can understand without a translator."

I look back to my grandfather's hologram as he smiles at me and says "Zaphora. What a beautiful woman you've become. And Zeke, you are quite the catch yourself young man. "

I shake my head in disbelief. There were scary campfire stories told about this type of technology.

My grandfather continues "I know you've been taught that all technology is bad for our Mother, but that's just not true. I was in my 40th year when The War of Venus began and in my 140th year when it ended so I remember how it was before and after the war changed life as we knew it. Before the war we had our share of technological advancements that hindered our ability to truly care and appreciate our Mother for all she does for us. We had machines that would fertilize the ground with chemicals that would make the food grow at a rate that we had never seen before. Allowing us to feed everyone on the planet many times over which ultimately cured hunger worldwide. This was great for a while, causing people to live longer, healthier lives without a shortage of goods. But that kind of manipulation to the skin of our Mother comes at a price. About 2 years after we developed this technology it started to kill our soil, making it infertile, and in turn making it increasingly harder to grow edible plants. This caused a war between the countries, over the few fertile pieces of land still available; more familiar to you as The War of Venus."

"It sounds like that technology started off helping humanity, but ended up turning us against each other. How do we know that this technology won't do the same?" I ask suspiciously.

"I know you have your doubts Zaphora, but trust me when I say that this is really my spirit, you're grandfather, speaking with you right now. How could this type of technology ever be wrong?"

"I guess you're right. But if there is nothing dangerous about this type of technology, why keep it a secret? Why not let everyone know it exists?"

"I wanted to, but your father was against it." Kanen interjects "He didn't want any technology in our village in fear that it might create another war. He was determined to ensure that we lead a life reaping only what we sowed from our Mother. And because he was my friend, I listened. I know how wrong that was now. Maybe with this the use of this technology, I don't know, maybe we could have prevented what happened to you Zeke." He says, lowering his head slightly.

"What do you mean?" Zeke finally says, breaking out of his stunned trance.

"While I was not in the woods the day you were taken, I can tell you that I believe it had to do with a meeting that I and the other tribe leaders had about ten years prior. If we had used this technology then we might have seen what was to come." He lowers his voice and continues "During this time we were right in the middle of a war with the inhabitants of The Dunes, a vicious clan that you, Zaphora, had the unpleasant fate of meeting in person."

I frown at that thought and think about how consistently unlucky I have been since I've turned 18.

"I don't understand. What does this have to do with what happened to me?" Zeke says.

"Allow me." My grandfather says. Kanen nods for him to continue and he does, "Our people migrated to the north after the war in hopes to live a simple life by becoming one with our Mother. We chose to take a few items from the old world that would not damage the Earth any further than we already had. There were, however, people who did not agree with this way of living. Those who believed that the War of Venus was not caused by humans and technology; but was the Mothers' way of cleansing the earth like she has done in the past with the dinosaurs. They refused to give up their technological advancements and chose to travel south in search of their own form of paradise."

"So why would they attack us? It seems like everyone would have been happy with the outcome." I say, puzzled.

"Well, after years of living underground, they were tired of the heat and animals that came with the climate that they chose to settle in. Travelers from their settlement begin to search for other places to live. Eventually stumbling upon our settlement in The Greenlands. Simply put, they wanted what we had, and would stop at nothing to get it. They were kidnapping our women and slaughtering our men at such a rapid rate that we began to run out of options. At the meeting I brought up earlier with the other elders, we were discussing the possibility of surviving outside of The Greenlands. Your father walked in late for the meeting with a tall, thin, regal gentlemen behind him. He introduced this man as Itan, the ruler of another tribe that lived on the other side of the woods. The other elders and I were skeptical of this considering we had been living on those lands for years and have never ran across anyone who looked anything like the man that was standing in front of us. But out of desperation we agreed to listen to his proposal for assistance." Kanen says.

"Did this man have glowing skin and pointy ears?" Zeke asks, interrupting the story.

"As a matter of fact he did. What an interesting observation Zeke." Kanen says, then continues where he left off. I can practically see the puzzle pieces falling together in Zeke's mind.

"He stated that he would protect our villages from any more harm with the use of a protection spell if we were willing to do something for him. Asta was suspicious of his offer and asked the gentleman to show us this spell that claims to be strong enough to hold back the creatures of The Dunes. Itan then demonstrated the spell for all of us, an invisible protective wall of some sort that only allowed villagers with our blood to pass through."

"Why did he want to help us and not the people of The Dunes?" I ask.

"He stated that our blood was pure, unlike the blood of the people who dwell in The Dunes. The spell would only work for those who are attached to nature; due to the fact that it relies on nature to be half of the defense."

"And what did he want from you?" Zeke asks.

"His conditions were that each tribe leader give their first born son to him once he reaches his 18th year, never to be contacted or heard from again. I voiced my concern that we should at least discuss this amongst ourselves away from the foreigner's ears before making a decision. Itan agreed, but before he left added that if we were able to come to a conclusion before sunrise, he would insure that we will be able to defend ourselves from this day forward by giving each tribe special ability to defend themselves with."

"Let me guess, the other leaders jumped to the chance to defend themselves and their tribe, even at the cost of their own child." Zeke says in a disappointing tone.

"I'm sad to report that this was the case. When I refused to do so, I was exiled with my tribe from The Greenlands and forced to find refuge outside the defense of Itan and his people." He says in a sad, reminiscing tone.

Zeke and I sit in silence taking in what we were just told. All of the lies. All of the hate directed at these poor people who were brave enough to stand up for the one thing my father never could. His family.

A solder appears on a screen on the wall interrupting our silence.

"Sir" he says saluting "I don't mean to interrupt you but you are needed in the war room."

"Thank you Zxian, I'll be right there."

The solder nods and the screen goes black again.

Kanen looks back over to us, studying each of our facial expressions before continuing. "I'm sorry but I'll have to cut this question and answer session short. If you have anything else you would like to discuss, I should be free in the morning after sunrise."

Zeke and I look up from the floor at him simultaneously and say "thank you."

Kanen nods "I'm always willing to help in any way that I can."

We all stand. Zeke and I stop briefly to say our goodbyes to our grandfather and long lost friends. We exit the compound and Kanen makes his way to the war room as we take a seat at the table I ate at earlier with Kameena.

"I need some air." Zeke says, before hopping out of his chair and darting towards the door.

"Zeke!" I yell as I go after him. When I make my way to the doorway I catch the back of him disappearing behind a house into the darkness. Santos and Tokala are laughing as they make their way to the Great Room and see the incident unfold. Tokala looks at me and then at Santos and says "Don't worry, I'll find him." and takes off behind Zeke.

Santos jogs up to me and places a hand on my shoulder. "Are you okay Zaphora? I know that was a lot of information to swallow."

"You can say that again. I just..... I just don't understand why my father would lie to me. We tell each other everything. At least I thought we did. And Zeke. How could he make a decision like that? How could he just tear apart our family?" I say as tears begin to stream down my cheeks.

"I know." he says embracing me and rubbing my back. "I'm sure he had his reasons. It's hard being the leader of so many people, especially during times of war. Hard decisions have to be made, for the good of everyone involved. "

"That's easy for you to say," I say as I pull away "you were lucky enough to never be put in this situation because your father chose you. He chose your family. That is the true definition of a leader to me. My father was a coward!"

"Zaphora, I know your upset, but just try, for a moment, just to look at things from his perspective. His world was crumbling around him. They just recovered from The War of Venus, and not long after, just when they thought that they were safe and life was beginning to feel normal again, they are attacked by the people of The Dunes, and brought into yet another war. His hands were tied. And I'm sad to say that I know how that feels." he says as he looks away.

"What? What do you mean you know how that feels? You've never had to choose your families happiness over that of your tribe!" I spit out.

"I'm just saying, I've been the leader of men. I know how it feels to make the hard decisions, that's all." We stand in silence for a moment, and then he says "I mean, didn't you have to take an oath to protect your tribe and do everything that you can to keep them safe and prospering?"

"What do you know of our oath?"

"You're oath?" he laughs "You really are naïve. The so called oath you claim ownership of belongs to us all, including members of my tribe. The first 8 tribe leaders established it when the Greenlands were founded to keep the people who survived from repeating the same mistakes. I thought they would at least tell you that much." he says, shaking his head.

"So you know of the oath, big deal. I just don't understand......I would never do what he did to us!" I shout.

"Well then what would you have done?"

"I don't know. Leave like your father did. Your tribe turned out okay without the help of the mystic stranger didn't it?"

"Well, not really. That was an option for us because we had the added advantage of the people from The Dunes attacking The Greenlands for a while before they realized where we were. And even with that added cover of protection, we lost some people on the journey to the mountains. Not to mention the people we lost after we arrived and drank the contaminated water. Our journey, by no means was a pleasant one. Our sacrifice was great, and still is. Your father didn't want that for you, for your people."

"I don't care how great the sacrifice was, we would have gotten through it together. Like he always taught me. How much of his teachings were a contradiction? How many lies have I been told?" I say, collapsing onto the steps and begin sobbing in my hands.

Santos comes back over to me and says "I'm sorry Zaphora. It's cold out here, let's get you inside." He picks me up with one motion and carries me inside. My eyes are so blurry from the tears and the pounding of my headache that I don't see how many halls we go down before reaching the guest room.

He slowly lays me on the bed and I curl up, facing the wall, and cry some more. He pulls a cover over me and leaves me to mourn my loss of innocence.

I cried for the first life I took. I cried for the loss of my beautiful locks (a symbol of our closeness and growing connection to The Mother). I cried for Zeke, and all that he has had to endure at the hands of my father. I cried for my forever shattered relationship with the closes man in my life. I cried until my eyes were dry and I had only my moaning and pain to keep me company.

Chapter 20

I wake up feeling like someone has sucked the life out of me. My head weighs 100 pounds and my stomach cries out for nourishment. I hear movement in the room and jump back to the headboard in defense.

"Zaphora, it's me." Zeke says in a low voice. "I'm sorry, I didn't mean to scare you. I just wanted to check on you. You've been sleep for quite some time."

I struggle to sit up on the bed before responding "How long have I been asleep?" I say, barely above a crackly whisper.

"A day and a half. I've been here most of the time, waiting for you to wake up. You would move around every now and then, moaning and screaming. What were you dreaming about?"

"I wish I could tell you. I can't remember anything from any of the dreams I had."

"Maybe that's a good thing." Zeke says, sitting on the bed next to me. "Do you want some food? You must be starving."

'Yes, that would be nice. Thank you." I say, resting my back on the wall next to me.

"Here" Zeke hands me a plate of berries, bread and cheese. "Eat up, you need your strength."

"Why? Where are we going?" I ask, stuffing some grapes into my mouth.

"Back to The Greenlands. I need to see our father." He says, furrowing his brow.

"I understand. When do we leave?"

"I was hoping to leave at sundown tomorrow if you are up for it. Santos and Tokala have agreed to come with us."

"I'm up for it. I should be back to normal by then." I say, thinking that I will never be back to that kind of normal again.

"Okay great." Zeke says as he stands "I'll leave you to your meal. I'll be out in the training center if you need me."

"Wait Zeke, are you okay? You ran away so quickly.....How are you handling all of this?"

"The best that I can I guess. I am over the anger of it. I just need closure now, which is why I want to go see our father. I need him to answer to what he has done so that I can let it go.

"Well I'm glad you're in a better place than you were a couple of nights ago."

"Talking about it helps. Tokala has really been like a brother to me throughout all of this. He helped me see that the anger was doing nothing but clouding my judgement, and that the sooner I forgive our father, the sooner that I can move on with my life."

"My, how you've matured!" I say with a grin.

"Well I am the oldest. It's my job to set a good example to my little sister, you know." he says tickling me. I almost spit out my food in laughter before he stops. He gets serious again and asks "But seriously, how are you? I was wrong for just running out on you the other day. I'm sorry for that Z."

"It's fine Zeke, I know you were hurting, so was I. Just don't do that to me again, okay? We are all we have in these foreign lands."

"I won't. The last thing I want is for you to feel like you can't talk to me." he says, shoving me playfully.

"Apology accepted. Now let me eat my food in peace." I say with a smile.

"Okay, okay. I'm leaving. I'll see you later." he says walking out the door.

I sit filling my empty stomach and taking in the beautiful decor. Two mahogany wooden chairs and a table anchor the room. An intricately woven red and gold rug covers the stone floor in front of my bed. Near the far wall is a large stone fireplace that seems to heat the massive room making the quilt on this bed I sit on nothing but decoration. The bed I sit on is large as well, able to sleep 4 adults comfortably.

The house maid has come in and out of the room about 5 times with more food and drinks until I have my fill. Giving me tea to help with my heavy head and prepping a tub for me to take a bath. Once I feel strong enough, I make my way to the bathroom, let my hair loose, and soak in the tub until my skin is wrinkled and the sun has set.

A fresh pair of clothes sits on a chair near the tub and I put them on without question. Tossing my old, and dirty clothes in the trash near the door. I dry my hair as much as I can and braid one single braid down the middle of my head.

I look at myself in the mirror and realize how much I have aged over such a short period of time. The eyes that used to be filled with excitement and wonder are now hardened and stern. The face that used to be smooth and youthful now bears the scars of battle. The body that used to be slim and nimble is now strong and muscular, causing the black hemp tank top and brown leather pants to fit tighter than I'm used to. I look down at my black leather boots, the last thing that reminds me of who I used to be, and smile. Feeling some happiness in the reminder of my old self.

The crisp air hits my face as I make my way over to the training center. Sharine runs up to me and hugs my waist "Hi Zaphora!" she says with a smile then darts off to play with some children near a makeshift fort.

"Zaphora, can I talk to you for a minute my dear?" Kamenna says, making her way over to me.

"Sure."

We sit on the steps of a nearby house before she continues.

"I know you've had to digest a lot of information in the last couple of days. I just wanted to check up on you and see how you've been doing."

"Thank you. I'm feeling better now. I'm sure Santos has told you that we plan to go back to The Greenlands to get some closure."

"That he did. And once you receive this closure you seek, what will you do then? Where will you live?"

"I...I don't know. I guess I haven't thought too much about that yet." I say, looking at my boots.

"Well, if you decide that you don't fit in at home anymore, you are more than welcome to start new here. Santos has told me how brave and fierce you are on the battlefield. We could always use a warrior like you in our army."

I think for a minute before responding. Although I know I won't fit at home anymore, I'm not so sure I would want to live out the rest of my life fighting someone else's battle either. This is probably what the snake in the desert meant about people using me for their advantage. I shake the thought out of my head and say "That is very generous of you, but I'm not quite sure I'm ready to jump in another battle so soon."

"Yes.....I figured you might say that." she says, studying me again. "Well, there was one more thing I wanted to discuss with you before you leave tomorrow. Kanen thinks you are not strong enough yet to receive all of the information that has been held from you, but I beg to differ. You are stronger than he thinks you are Zaphora."

"All of the information?" I say, more alert now to the conversation "What do you mean all of the information?"

"Well, there was one thing that Kanen didn't tell you yesterday.......Aquene is not your real mother."

Chapter 21

"Why ……Why would you tell such a hurtful lie? Just to get me to stay? How dare you!" I say, standing.

"No lies here Zaphora." Kamenna says, slowly standing with me "I have no reason to lie to you. I just feel that you have been kept in the dark for too long. My intention is only to shine a light on the truth."

Kanen walks up to us as she finishes her statement and says "Kamenna, please tell me that you just didn't do what I told you not to do!"

"Now Kanen, you know I don't believe in secrets. The girl had a right to know the truth." She says, glaring at me again. Those sneaky eyes burrowing into my soul.

"Yes, but not by you. Not like this!" He snaps back.

"So…. She's telling the truth? The only mother I have ever known is not my mother?" I ask Kanen.

"I'm afraid so my dear. This is not how I wanted you to find out though," He says looking sternly at Kamenna, then back at me "But she speaks the truth."

My world begins to spin and my dinner comes flying out of my mouth before I can think. A weightless feeling overcomes me and I pass out.

When I come to I am lying on my back with Kanen and Kamenna standing over me.

"Are you okay my dear? That was quite a fall." he says, helping me up off the ground.

"I'll be fine. I just don't want to be lied to anymore. Why didn't you tell me this when you spoke to my brother and I a couple of days ago?" I say, looking at Kanen.

"I'm sorry Zaphora. I didn't think you were ready to know. You have been through so much...I"

"I'm tired of people treating me like I'm some fragile child. I almost died! Several times! So I have no interest in living a life that is a lie. If you have any respect for me at all, you will tell me the truth. ALL of the truth. And not leave anything out this time." I say sternly.

"You're right. You have the right to know, and I will tell you everything I know." He says, looking remorseful.

I follow him back to the room with the calming green light where we had our first discussion and he begins to tell me all that he knows. He tells me that my father was in love with a woman from another land that he met on his 15th year while hunting in the forest. He said that this woman, Inka, was what our people called Elves, because they had features similar to that of Elves in old stories and fairytales; Long stark black hair, golden brown skin, pointy ears, and ash gray eyes. My father fell madly in love with her and they began sneaking to see each other at night when it was safe for both of them to get away. One night he went to the forest to meet Inka and she never showed. This lasted for months before my father realized that she was never coming back. He was devastated. His first love was gone without a trace and there was no way to find her. Two years later, on his 17th year, he was married to Aquene through an arranged marriage between their tribes, and they had Zeke a year later. One day, when my father was hunting in the woods for food, Inka showed up telling him of her travels and how much she missed him. Although he was angry at her for leaving without a word, his heart overtook his logic and they began sneaking away together once a week again. One afternoon Inka was followed by her brother who disapproved of the union and banned her from ever seeing him again. Zeke fell into a deep depression that lasted for about a year until Kanen gave him a long talk about his responsibilities to his village, and most importantly, his family. He had all but put his romance with Inka in the past when her father, Itan, showed up with me in hand and a pact to protect our tribes from the people of The Dunes in exchange for my protection and the first born son of each tribe leader on their 18th year. My father agreed to this trade and has been taking care of me ever since.

"So you're telling me that my real mother is an Elvin woman named Inka? And that my Elvin grandfather, Itan, is responsible for making my life, and the life of my family the hell that it is now?" I say, standing in anger.

"Well, that's one way to look at it." Kanen says in a calm tone.

"That's the only way to look at it!" I say, almost screaming.

"Zaphora is right Kanen. The sooner you stop sugar coating and letting her stand in her truth, the stronger she will be. She's not a child anymore, and she needs to know that this world isn't all butterflies and lilies." Kamenna says.

"Thank you Kamenna, for treating me like the woman I am. And thank you Kanen, for telling me the whole truth about myself and my father. If you two will excuse me, I would really like to be alone with my thoughts right now." I say.

"Of course." They both say in unison.

I leave the room feeling suffocated and decide to take a walk around the mountains to try to regain some clarity.

I walk the dusty path that leads to the gate and get stopped as I try to exit.

"I'm sorry miss. It's too dangerous out there for us to let you out right now. The gates will be open again at dawn." A tall, green eyed solder says as I approach.

"Too dangerous!" I say, and laugh hysterically at the thought.

"Josef, its fine. I'll look out for her." A baritone voice says from behind me.

"I don't need anyone to...." I start and turn to see that it's Santos.

"No problem Santos." Josef says and opens the gates for us.

I walk out, arms crossed, in front of Santos and he jogs to catch up.

"I don't need you to babysit me Santos!" I say, staring ahead.

"I know. But I also knew they wouldn't let you out of that gate unless I came with you. So just act like I'm not here." he retorts.

"That's kind of hard to do with your big feet shaking the ground behind me."

He laughs a little at this which makes me crack a smile, then says "Well, we can't all walk as elegantly as you princess Zaphora."

I try to compose my smirk and shoot him a look of disdain.

"I know a great place to clear your mind. Let me show you." He says, and swoops me over his shoulder before I can oppose.

He carries me up the side of the mountain until we reach the top. Nothing but air and rocks are this high, and the feeling of being away from the world makes my whole being exhale.

"It's beautiful up here." I say, as he puts me down. I find a smooth rock near the edge of the cliff and take a seat.

Santos sits next to me before saying "I found it shortly after we decided to settle here. Some of my tribe members started to become sick and die off from the water. It was all too much for me to handle so I use to spend hours up here away from it all. It made it easier to cope with the deaths I guess."

I look over at him unsure of what to say to that, so I just say "I'm sorry."

"It's fine. I'm healed from it now and I believe being here had a lot to do with that healing, that's why I'm sharing it with you."

We sit in our silence for a long while after that. Listening to the wind. To our thoughts. To our heartbeats.

"I wish I could just live here." I say, exhaling the fresh air.

"Now that would do the world a great injustice. Zaphora, the daughter of a great tribe leader and Elvin woman, living the rest of her days at the top of a mountain like some outcast. Mother Earth simply would not allow it." he says, winking at me.

"Very funny." I smirk at him "I'm trying to be serious right now. I just found out my world is falling apart!"

"I know, but how long will you play the victim in all of this. I know you're hurting, and you have that right, but we've all been through things. Your brother was taken from your village on his 18th year, and walked all the way here, dehydrated, hungry and tired, on the word of another. Only thinking of what you should be thinking of right now. He is free. You are free Zaphora!" He says, standing with conviction. "There is no one holding you captive. Feeding you scraps. Forcing you to fight for your life. You've survived the worse of it. So live! Show me that saving you is the best thing that I will ever do." he says, looking into my eyes.

The tears I have been clinging to come spilling from my eyes at once. He was right. I'm alive. I'm free. And I'm still ungrateful. Still selfish. Still worried about only my own issues.

Who did I think I was demanding the truth from Kanen? If not for the respect he has for my father I probably would be locked in a cage somewhere right now.

And my brother. My poor brother has found out that he was betrayed by the man that raised him and doesn't even know that the man that he was given to was his grandfather.

And Santos. My voice of reason. A man who risked his life for me more times than I can count. And has agreed, after being away from his own home and family for years, to follow me and my brother on our journey back home.

I spring to my feet at this thought and wrap my arms around his neck. Hanging there for a couple of moments until he wraps his arms around my back to return the embrace.

"Thank you." I whisper in his ear and pull away.

He pulls away too but doesn't let go of me, instead he leans in and kisses my forehead gently.

I look into his eyes as butterflies dance in my stomach. His warm breath heats my face sends a chill down my spine. The energy between us is magnifying and pulls us together, mouth to mouth. Time stops, and for a short moment in time, everything is perfect.

Chapter 22

The night air is crisp and calming, regenerating my spirit with every inhalation. It's been hours since Santos left me to my thoughts at the top of the mountain. The kiss we shared has changed the dynamic between us. And though it's a beautiful distraction, it's a distraction all the same; and now is the time for focus.

I began meditating about an hour ago. An exercise I haven't performed since my brother was taken, so it's taken longer than usual for me to quiet all of the voices in my head and tap into my spirit. Once I do, I begin immediately to cleanse and balance all of my chakras. I reach my crown chakra and something happens that has never happened before, I start to feel myself levitate. A feeling that I thought would scare me, but has done the opposite. Intriguing me. Creating a wanting for more. I go deeper into my spirit, and what I assume is higher off of the ground because the wind is increasing as I elevate.

Images flood my mind like a slideshow I don't quite understand.

A crying baby with gray eyes in a wooden crib laced with vines.

A woman with long black hair crying and holding the baby.

A little girl walking through the forest with an older man with pointy ears.

The same little girl playing with my father.

My father teaching me how to fish.

My brother teaching me how to hunt.

My first battle in The Dunes.

My reunion with my brother.

My first kiss with Santos.

Then Light. Bright white light.

Refusing to open my eyes and give into the lightheaded feeling that is overtaking me, I concentrate harder. Travel deeper.

Out of the light comes another picture.

Ferocious African wild dogs attacking me.

Blood everywhere.

Zeke passed out and bleeding on the sand.

My eyes open and I drop to the ground. Sweat soaks my clothes and drips from my face. My senses start to return and my body begins to freeze. I must find cover.

I drag my deflated body into a small crevice in the mountain side and lay there.

My erratic heartbeat takes away any since of serenity that I may have achieved over the last couple of hours. A spider crawls over my leg but I'm too tired to care.

Zeke. I can't lose him again. I hear Shakira's voice '*The only choice you have in the matter is if you will take part in your history*'.

Does that mean I can change what I saw? Of course I can! I can change this. I control my destiny, not some vision. I can be stronger. Better. I can make sure that Zeke doesn't succumb to such a fate. Even if it is at the risk of losing my own life.

I force myself off the ground and stretch a little before heading back. The earth beneath my feet takes on a new feel as I run with a purpose. I will train day and night if I have to. My brother will no longer bear the burden of my sins. I won't allow it.

A growing cloud of fog before me stops me dead in my tracks. I don't have time for this right now. Scanning the fog, there is no sign of the dark figure so I decide to jog cautiously through until I get to the gates. The fog climbs so high above me and becomes so thick that I can no longer see in front of me. A cold hand touches my shoulder and I turn to see the dark figure standing behind me.

"Zaphora……….Come to me Zaphora……….." it says and floats backwards, away from me.

I try to turn and run but my body stiffens and I begin being pulled toward him, deeper into the fog. The deeper I go, the more fog I inhale, the slower my breathing becomes.

"Zaphora………….This way Zaphora……….." The deep and haunting voice beckons to me.

My head gets lighter, and the muscles in my body relax. My eyelids are heavy and wants to give into this sleepy feeling. I prepare myself to hit the ground when I feel the pressure of claws on my shoulders.

"Zaphora………No………" the voice screeches after me as I rise higher into the sky. My heavy head manages to look up at the huge hawk holding me by the shoulders before I completely pass out.

The searing pain of my right temple forces me into consciousness. My eyes are crusted over and unable to open. My hands immediately go to work clearing the obstruction of my vision.

"Careful Zaphora. Allow me." A familiar voice says in the darkness.

"Makiya? Is that you?" I ask, fearing that my ears deceive me.

"Yes Zaphora, It's me. Now hold still so I can remove the medicine from your eyes."

I do as he says and he uses a cloth covered in warm water to wipe my eyes clean. When he finishes, I open my eyes to see a chandelier made of bones hanging over me. As my vision clears I see tall candles with dancing blue fire inside of the chandelier.

"What…What is this place?" I say sitting up on the wooden table.

"Welcome to my humble abode Zaphora. So nice we could finally meet." A tall, dark man, with glowing ash gray eyes says as he creeps out of the shadow in the corner of the room.

I study him carefully. His shaved head reveals dark tribal markings on his scalp and a row of earrings in his ears. His tight black leather pants match a long leather coat that hangs loosely from his small frame.

"Are you Itan?" I ask cautiously.

"Oh, heavens no. I understand that we are both old Elvin men but I am nothing like that power hungry degenerate. I am Drakko the Inferno. This is my mountain that you have been staying at for the past couple of days." he says with a slight smirk.

"These mountains belong to the Sililoquii tribe, why are you claiming them as your own?" I ask, standing slowly.

"Wrong again my dear. That's two for two. This has been my mountain for hundreds of years. The Sililoquii tribe only began to live here because I allowed them to. Figured it was time for me to start socializing a little with humanity again." he says with a chuckle "And they were only allowed to stay here because I knew that eventually you would arrive if they did. And here you are. So I suppose they have you to thank for their current living situation." He finishes, sitting on a large chair that is also made of bones. I gather the bones are from a creature that no longer exists because they are so huge.

"What do you mean they have me to thank. How do you know who I am? "

"Let's just say me and your mother, you're real mother, were very close once. And I promised her that I would look out for you, so that's what I did."

"You know my real mother? Who is she? Where is she?"

"So many questions. You're an eager one aren't you?" he says, sizing me up. "Yes I know your real mother. You look so much like her. And have a lot of her same feistiness." he laughs, and continues "She was here not too long ago, actually. She told me that her father has been looking for you. Something about how your blood is stronger than human blood because it is mixed with Elvin blood, so he could feed off of you, and you alone, and live forever."

"Wait what? So the figure that was following me in the fog is Itan?" I say, shaking my head at the new information. "So where is she now? Why didn't she wait for me if she knew I was coming?"

"She had a couple of things to take care of back at The Shrine before she met up with you again. Which is why she asked me to watch out for you."

"The Shrine. Is that were your people are from?"

"Yes. And currently they are undergoing what your civilization would call a civil war. She went back to stop her father and his power hungry clan before they end up destroying The Shrine for good."

"Why aren't you there helping your people with her?"

"They stopped being my people a long time ago Zaphora. I no longer take sides in battles of power. When you've lived as long as I have, you realize that power is just an illusion. Everyone chases it and no one truly finds it. I prefer to live the rest of my days outside of that rat race. In the peaceful dwelling that is this mountain." he says, stretching his long arms to emphasize his home. "I only agreed to look out for you out of the love I have for your mother, nothing more."

"Well thank you. I know that you didn't want to get involved in my mess but I appreciate the fact that you did."

"You are most welcome my dearest Zaphora." He says standing and bowing to me. He then makes his way over to a counter and pours himself a drink. "Can I get you something to ease your troubles?" he says, holding the drink out to me.

"I'll pass, thank you." Thinking of the last time I had a drink I didn't recognize. "And what role do you play in all of this?" I say, turning my attention over to Makiya.

"I've been watching out for you since the day you left for your spirit journey. That same night I was awoken by a vision of you trapped in the middle of a thick fog, screaming in agony. I knew then that I had to find you and do all I could to ensure your safety." He walks closer to me and continues "What I didn't tell you before, because we ran out of time, was that my spirit journey reviled to me the ability to shape shift into a hawk."

I think back and remember all of the times I remembered seeing a hawk soar above me on my journey.

"So that was you above me that day by the lake? And the day in the desert when I was tied to the tree?"

"Indeed. And last night in the fog before you passed out."

"Well thank you for getting me out of there, although I could have used your assistance when I was kidnapped." I say, giving him the side eye.

"I wanted to. Believe me I did. But I was given strict instructions by Shakira when I went on my spirit journey not to interfere with yours. I wouldn't have interfered this last time but I Itan was trying to take you with him and something in me snapped. I couldn't just let you get abducted a second time, no matter what the consequences are. I couldn't live with myself is something happened to you and I could have done something to stop it."

His statement adds extra weight to my already overloaded heart. Yet another person has risked their life for my survival. Another debt I'll probably never get to repay. And for what? A weak, scared, lost little girl with more problems than solutions. What's the point?

"Thank you Mikaya. You're loyalty and friendship means a lot to me."

"Don't mention it." He says with a shy shrug.

"So how do you two know each other in the first place?" I ask.

"I was following you when you were taken to The Dunes when you went underground and I lost you." Makiya says "I was circling the compound for weeks looking for a way to get in when your mother came to me in a vision and told me that you were on your way here. When I arrived she was leaving, but not before introducing me to Drakko, and saying that we were to look out for you. I've been here ever since."

"That he has." Drakko says with an irritated sigh. He takes a large sip from his smoking drink before continuing. "But now that the two of you are reunited, and I have held up my end of the deal, you can be on your way." He says, rising off of his chair and ushering us towards the door.

Chapter 23

"Good luck on your journey, I wish I could say that it's been a pleasure, but…." Drakko slams the door in our face and the wind causes me to stumble a bit. Makiya catches my arm and steadies me "That's two for two Zaphora" he says in a voice like Drakko's, referring to the last time he caught me before I fell and we both laugh.

"What was his problem?" I say, making my way down the mountain.

"I think he was fed up with all of our questions." He says, following behind me. "Before you got here I had been here for about a month waiting for you to arrive. I've been through my share of unnatural occurrences, being that my tribe is known for its connection to the spirit world, but I have never encountered anyone as strange as Drakko."

"What do you mean?" I ask, intrigued.

"Well, from what I've gathered, he's like your mother in terms of being Elvin. But his aura is non-existent. Like he's dead or something. And his face. You heard him say that he has been living in these mountains for hundreds of years, yet he looks no older than you or I. How is that possible?"

"Yes, that is strange." I say, thinking of how much I still I don't know about that side of my family. I make a mental note to find my mother after my trip to The Greenlands to confront my father.

"And do you know why they call him Drakko the Inferno?" Makiya says, in his usual inquisitive tone. Reminding me of how much he used to retain without even trying when we attended class together. He has always been a soul that yearned for adventure and information. I shouldn't be surprised that he decided to follow me. It's in his nature.

"No, Why?" I ask.

"Because he is pyro kinetic! He has the ability to control and create fire with his mind. And not just any kind of fire, blue fire! Have you ever heard of such a thing? It was fascinating to watch. I wish you were there with me to witness it in action. I can't think of anyone else that would have enjoyed it as much as I did." He says looking into my eyes and smiling that wide smile that brings out his dimples.

My face gets hot and I try to think of something, anything that will take the spotlight off of me.

"Well, I think your gift is equally as fascinating Makiya. When did you find out that you were able to morph into a Hawk?" Yes, good change of subject Zaphora!

"I would say that my complete transformation took place on my 19th year. But little things would happen that lead up to that transformation during my 18th year."

"Like what?"

"Like I would be training and wings would sprout from my back, or feathers would sprout from my head. It was a very strange time in my life. I'm just glad that most of the awkward stuff happened while I was alone on spirit journey." He says with a chuckle.

"Wow that does sound uncomfortable." I say, remembering the strange changes I've also been going through this year.

"So, where are we headed?" He asks, changing the subject.

"Back to the Silliloquii tribes' headquarters. I was going to try to train a little and get some rest before the trip back to The Greenlands tomorrow. You are more than welcome to fly back home if you'd like though. You've already done more for me than I could ever repay you for." I say, looking back at him.

"Nonsense!" He says, cutting in front of me and stopping me in my tracks. "You're my friend Zaphora. There will never be a need for you to repay me. I was only doing what any friend would do. You would have done the same." He says, placing a hand on my shoulder.

A shiver tickles my spine at his touch. What is happening to me?

"And if it's all the same with you, I would prefer to make sure you make it back to The Greenlands before we part ways again."

I divert my eyes to my boots and wipe my sweaty palms on my pants before responding "That would be great."

"Great." He says, before dropping his hand and walking in front of me.

I watch his broad shoulders descend the mountain and remember Santos. It's going to be a longer night than I thought.

Chapter 24

We make it back to the gate right before sundown and are greeted by Tokala and a heavy set solder guarding the camp.

"Where have you been?" Tokala says as he runs to me and swallows me with his embrace. "We've been looking for you all day!"

"Not very hard I see." I say, jokingly. "It's a long story. Tokala, this is Makiya, he's a friend from The Greenlands. Makiya, this is Tokala, he's the jokester of the Silliloquii tribe."

"Nice to meet you Tokala" Makiya says, shaking Tokala's hand.

"You too. Any friend of Zaphora's is a friend of ours. And Jokester?" He says looking at me from the corner of his eyes "I'll show you a Jokester." He says, tossing me over his shoulder like a sack of flour.
 I kick and flail around in his arms with no avail while Makiya follows behind, laughing hysterically.
He carries me until we make it to the room with the two big chairs that Kameena took me to when I first arrived to their village.

"I found the missing person and would like my reward." Tokala shouts as he enters the room and sets me on the concrete floor.

Makiya is still laughing behind me as I regain my balance and shove Tokala. I look over to see Santos, Kanen, Zeke and Kameena filing out of the room to the right.

"Zaphora!" Zeke shouts and runs over to me, picking me off the ground with his hug. "Where have you been? We've been searching for you."

"I know. I apologize for the scare. I'm fine though. It's a long story. I'll tell you on our trip back to The Greenlands." I say, with a smile. "Everyone, this is Makiya, he is a friend from the Greenlands. Makiya, this is Kanen and Kameena, the leaders of the Silliloquii tribe. Santos. And I believe you know my brother Zeke."

"Zeke!" Makiya says, embracing him. "I thought you were dead! Where have you been man?"

"That too is a long story" Zeke says smirking over at me "I'll tell you over dinner. You must be starving."

"I am actually." Makiya says, holding his stomach.

"Well don't be shy" Kameena says "Please, follow me, we'll get you nice and full before your long trip."

"Thank you! It's nice to meet all of you." Makiya says, and starts catching up with Zeke as they follow Kameena into the next room.

"Come son," Kanen says to Tokala, "I need to go over some strategies with you in the war room before you leave. Zaphora, I'm glad you're safe my dear." He says, kissing my hand. Santos gives him a look of irritation and Kanen and Tokala laugh and make their way back into the room to the right, shutting the door behind them.

Santos's strong embrace takes me by surprise. His woodsy aroma invades my senses and quickens my heartbeat. "Don't ever scare me like that again." He whispers into my ear and kisses me passionately before I can reply.

"I won't." I say quietly.

We walk to a quiet spot near the edge of the village and sit on a broken log next to the lake. I tell him of the adventure I had while I was away and information I discovered in my missing hours. I choose to leave out what I learned during my meditation in the mountains, not wanting him to worry about me more than he already does. He agrees that I should go to look for my mother after seeing my father and says he will come with me.

He then tells me that his father says that an informant they have planted in The Dunes sends word that their people are running out of food. I tell him that this information is nothing new. That the people of The Dunes have been struggling to survive for years now. He states that this time they are on the verge of starvation. Having exhausted most of the edible plants and animals in the desert. Some have even resulted to cannibalism. He says that they have started sending groups of their strongest people out to find a more habitable place to live.

The thought of this frightens me to my core. The Silliloquii are more than capable of defending themselves from an invasion, but I'm not so sure about my people in The Greenlands. My father made that deal with Itan years ago because we weren't able to defend ourselves then. And the years have brought more women and children than abled-bodied warriors to fight battles with. On top of that, now that Zeke has escaped, I'm pretty sure Itan has withdrawn his wall of protection, leaving my unsuspecting family and friends vulnerable to whatever kinds of madness they end up bringing there way.

"What will my people do? We can't survive that kind of invasion. And without the protection spell from Itan, they will surely take over my lands and enslave my people."

"Don't worry Zaphora. We'll find a way to fight them off. Maybe your mother can help." Santos replies, trying to reassure me.

"Yes, maybe." I say, not as confident in the plan.

I decide to focus less on the future events and return to the present; Immersing myself into this moment in time. I place my head on Santos's muscular arm and he lifts it, pulling me into his comfort. We sit for a long time, just watching the lake as the wind sends ripples through the water.

A gust of wind chills my face and I open my eyes to Santos carrying me in his arms. He looks down at me with a comforting smile and kisses me on the forehead.

"Did I fall asleep?" I ask, smiling back at him.

"Yes, I didn't want to wake you." He says, placing me on the bed. "Get some sleep. We have a long day ahead of us tomorrow."

"Goodnight" I say, pulling the covers over myself.

"Goodnight Zaphora." He says, closing the door behind him.

The sun warms my face as I open my eyes to the willow trees swaying above me. The bed of yellow pansy's bring me great cushion as I inhale the crisp air that surrounds me. A black crow flies over me, perching itself on a nearby tree branch. The crow eyeballs me with contempt causing a feeling of uneasiness to overcome me. It opens his mouth and thick smoke pours out, slowly covering the bed of flowers beneath me. I jump up at the touch of the fog that chills my skin and begin to run quickly through the field. *"Zaphoraaaaa .... You'll never escape me Zaphora................ You WILL be mines... "* an eerie voice calls behind me. The sound of a flowing stream ahead pushes me to run even faster to try to escape this entity. I reach the stream and dive in without a second thought. I grab onto the nearest form of plant life that I can find and hold my breath as I look up to the top of the stream. The fog seems to thicken above the stream, blocking out any sunshine that did exist above me. The plant life begins to grab my legs and arms, holding me under water. A dark liquid seeps into the water, stopping right before my face.

I jerk awake with my chest rising and falling with every harsh breath. Pulling the sweat soaked covers from my body sends pain signals to my brain. The glow of the moon lights a path across the stone floor as I make my way to the bathroom. My altered skin pigment in the mirror makes me shudder as I remember Shakira's words *'These figures are unable to harm you in reality, but can do so in your dreams.'*

I won't let him brake me. I won't give him that power.

Before I know it, I'm lacing my boots and flying out the door to the training center. It's the middle of the night so I'm training by myself for a while before anyone joins me. And when they do, I barely notice. I have tunnel vision.

Itan's face is on every target. On every warrior I spar with. It gets so intense at one point that I am only allowed to train with the dummies because I almost cut off the arm with a guard I was sparing with.

I train in everything from sword fighting to hand to hand combat. Sharpening my skills and working my muscles until the middle of the afternoon before I take a break to eat.

Lunch consists of some sort of stew and blueberry tea. Santos, Tokala, Zeke and Makiya join me in the middle of my meal to discuss the route that we will take back to The Greenlands. We decide to leave tonight when the temperatures are cooler and easier to manage. Tokala pulls out a map that their people made to plot out the surrounding area and says we should take the mountain path for as long as we can before taking the desert path. Being that the mountain gives more concealment, and the people of The Dunes are out roaming the lands, we agree that this is the best plan and agree to leave when the moon is over the house furthest to the north.

After lunch I retreated back to the training center to practice some more with Zeke. We spared and practiced some knife throwing. He beamed at how advanced I'd become since the last time we trained together. After a couple of hour we both decide to rest a little before our long journey.

Kameena has one of her housemaids draw a bath for me when I make it back to my room.

"One of my merchants came across this when he was exchanging items with a nomad. I believe it belongs to you." She hands me a pouch with the pocket knives my father had made for me before I started my spirit journey. The flicker of the torchlight dancing playfully on the carefully crafted Z on the handles brings a tear to my eye.

"Thank you Kameena. You don't know how much this means to me."

"I'm happy to provide you with a glimmer of happiness in such a challenging time in your life. I brought these for you as well." She places a bag with some of her clothes, herbs, and fruit on the bed. "I'll see you for supper." She says, and leaves the room, closing the door behind her.

Holding the blades close to my chest I try to hold onto the memory of simpler times. Before lies, kidnappings, and strange figures in the fog became my reality. Vowing to myself that once I leave this room, I will also leave behind the illusion that I was ever safe. That world was a fantasy. This is my reality now. For better or worse, I'm wide awake now.